THE JOURNEYMAN

ELIZABETH YATES

Edited by Gloria Repp

Original title
Patterns on the Wall

GREENVILLE, SOUTH CAROLINA

The Journeyman

Project Editor
Wanda Sutton

Cover and illustrations
Stephanie True

© 1943 Elizabeth Yates
© 1990 Bob Jones University Press
Greenville, South Carolina 29614

ISBN 0-89084-535-2
Printed in the United States of America

20   19   18   17   16   15   14   13

Books for Young People by Elizabeth Yates

Amos Fortune, Free Man
Someday You'll Write
Sam's Secret Journal
Prudence Crandall
With Pipe, Paddle, and Song
Sarah Whitcher's Story
We, the People
Carolina's Courage
The Journeyman

Acknowledgments

My sincere thanks are due to the following for their help given me while gathering information for this book: to Thelma Brackett, State Librarian, Concord, New Hampshire, who guided my search through a multitude of early newspaper files, local histories, and other books; to Donald Tuttle, New Hampshire State Planning and Development Commission, for his interest and enthusiasm in uncovering data concerning "eighteen-hundred-and-froze-to-death"; and to Robb Sagendorph, publisher of *The Old Farmer's Almanac,* for his kindness in putting at my disposal files of *The Old Farmer's Almanac* to confirm weather conditions in 1816.

E.Y.

Publisher's Note

During the first quarter of the nineteenth century, itinerant peddlers and journeymen crisscrossed the New England states carrying news, opening up the frontier, and supplying commodities of every description. Jared Austin, journeyman painter, is representative of a class of workmen who were brave and practical and instinctively artistic.

Jared had long been enthralled with the beauty of God's creation. The glory of color and design that he saw in nature flamed in his heart, and he sought to reproduce it in his art. With his paints, brushes, and stencils, he traveled the countryside, bringing beauty to the homes of the sturdy New England farmers–beauty that would cheer and hearten them even through the bleak winter months.

The year of 1816 will long be remembered in New England as "eighteen-hundred-and-froze-to-death," when late frosts destroyed crops and snow fell every month of the year. The bitter weather was not limited to New England, however. From Ireland, England, and France came reports of the spring being the latest ever known, of few trees in bloom, of scanty vegetation.

Astronomers of the day discovered black spots on the sun's disk and thought that this phenomenon accounted for the extraordinary changes in the weather. Recent scientific studies suggest that the eruption in 1815 of a massive volcano, Mount Tambora in Indonesia, caused a cloud of volcanic dust that was responsible for the unusual cold.

For Jared Austin, however, the endless winter brought more than cold and frost: he became the community's scapegoat and the focus of a witch hunt. The attack was led by a small group of "tavern haunters," lazy and superstitious farmers who had given up the grim struggle with the weather and spent their days gossiping at the local inn. Jared's victory over their accusations was a result of his determination to refute a lie rather than to run from it and his quiet faith in a God Who sends storms as well as sunshine.

Chapter One

Jared lay on his back, watching the boughs above him sway against the spring sky. They made a pattern of green upon blue that repeated itself down the brook, through the woods, along the roadside–wherever there were trees to move against the sky.

Searching around in the grass, he found a large soft leaf and laid it on a stone. With a sharp piece of iron which he kept in his pocket, he made cutouts on the leaf until his design roughly resembled the lacy pattern he had been looking at overhead. He pressed the leaf on a flat stone from the brook and then smeared thin streaks of red clay in the openings. After letting the clay dry, he carefully lifted the leaf and studied the stencil on the stone.

He was so interested in what he was doing that he had not noticed a girl coming across the pasture on the other side of the brook, a girl with bare feet and dark brown hair that lay on her shoulders. Jennet Thaxter stood and watched for a moment, her homespun dress whipped against her sturdy legs by the spring wind.

"Jared Austin, are you making pictures again?" she asked.

Jared gave no answer. He did not seem surprised at the sound of a voice across the brook when he might have thought himself alone in the pasture. He smiled at the design on the stone and then spoke without looking up.

"I'm not making pictures, Jennet, I'm making beauty. See–" He held up the stone, and Jennet leaned across the brook to look at it.

She screwed up her eyes but could make nothing out of the streaky red lines across the surface of the stone; so she shook her head vigorously and her dark hair swirled in the wind.

"It's nothing at all that I can see," she said.

Jared looked up at the boughs overhead. "See those leaves against the sky? I want to make that same kind of beauty."

Jennet laughed. "I'd rather look up at the trees."

"But you can't always look at the trees," Jared replied quickly. "Winter comes when there are no leaves. Night comes when there is no light. But if I make a design like the design the boughs make against the sky, it could be repeated anywhere, and you could always have beauty."

Jennet shook her head. "We're farming folk, Jared. We have no time for things like that. Something dreadful happens to people who waste time; something dreadful will happen to you. I've heard my father and mother talk about you. They say they don't know what you'll come to."

"Neither do I," Jared said with a smile.

Jennet sat on a rock by the brook and edged her bare feet into the moving water. "It's cold!" she exclaimed, drawing her feet back and tucking them under her rough blue dress.

"There's snow on the mountains still."

"I mustn't stay," Jennet said, but she made no move to go. "I was sent to fetch the cows home; it's near milking time."

Jared looked across the brook and into Jennet's eyes. "Jennet, when I'm grown a man will you marry me?"

Jennet surveyed him appraisingly–earnest gray eyes, pale face and sandy hair, lean small body which was no bigger than hers, though he was a year older. Then her gaze shifted to his hands as he trailed them in the brook. The water slipping around his fingers made them look long and very thin.

"No," she said deliberately. She'd always said that the man she'd marry would be a strong, young farmer with a hundred acres in his own name and every one of them under tillage.

She waited before saying more. She had found with the boys in the village who asked that question that if she waited long enough, they would answer back, "All right, I'll find someone else," and then she could say, "So shall I," and that was the beginning of such a toss-about of words as might end any way the more witty cared to have them end.

Finally Jennet glanced up from watching his hand in the water and looked at Jared. His eyes were straight on her. At their clear glance, Jennet felt ashamed for a moment, ashamed of trying to banter with him as she would with other boys. Jared was not like other boys. Something made him different.

She opened her lips to speak, and then from the hill behind them came the sharp, impatient sound of a man's voice calling Jared. The boy stood up quickly.

"I must go–it's my father." He shivered.

Jennet held out her hand to him across the brook. Jared reached for it, but the brook was too wide and even their finger tips would not touch.

"I shouldn't have asked you to marry me, Jennet," Jared said gently. "You're worth someone fine and fearless. I'm not that, am I?"

Then the voice boomed over the hillside again, and this time Jared turned and darted up the steep slope. Jennet stood still, watching him.

Lying where he had left it was the stencil on the stone. Jennet crossed the water and picked it up. She looked at it and then at the small leaves interlacing overhead.

"It is beautiful," she said to herself and waded back to the other side.

Jared stood before his father, thin and white and obedient. The man, towering above the boy, said nothing. His lips were set in a hard line; his eyes had narrowed with anger. The boy stood firmly, waiting for one brave moment before his father's arm was raised, knowing that at the first blow he would crumple under it. He had learned long ago not to cry out. But the blow did not fall. Then Jared saw–standing behind his father–a stranger with a horse.

"Take the horse to the barn and bed him for the night," Eben Austin said, turning abruptly.

Jared approached the horse and put his hand on the bridle; then he stole a brief glance up at the man whose presence had saved him a beating. He was a tall man, journey-stained, and a smile crossed his face at the boy's swift glance. Then the two men started toward the house, and Jared led the horse to the barn.

There was always a stall for a traveler's horse, and it was always bedded and waiting. Jared slipped the bridle off and patted the heavy-boned head. He brought an armful of hay and the horse sank her soft muzzle into it. The boy turned to remove the saddle and then stood still to examine it, for it was like no saddle he had ever seen before.

Attached to it, where saddlebags usually hung, was a leather apron consisting of many pockets, and in each pocket was a brush. The brushes were of varying sizes and thick-nesses, and near the handle of each one were small rims of color where the paint had not come away. Below the brush pockets were flat plackets of dried pigments waiting to be made into paint. Jared looked in one and found an envelope of blue powder, in another, green, and in another, yellowish-orange ocher. The stranger must be a journeyman painter, he thought with delight. He lifted the saddle carefully and set it over against the wall. Then, after making sure that the horse had all it needed for comfort, he turned and went to-ward the house.

A traveler was a welcome person in that remote country-side. He was housed for as long as he would stay, his horse was stabled or turned out to pasture, and no payment was thought of save the tales he had gleaned in his journeying. The hard work of farming the boulder-strewn fields always slackened apace at the arrival of a traveler, an extra big back-log blazed on the hearth in his honor, and extra food was set on the table. Seated together on the settle, the stranger and Eben Austin were soon filling the room with words, as stew simmered in an iron pot on the hob.

Jared's stepmother was standing by the wide fireplace, one hand stirring the pot, the other rocking the cradle of the baby. Two young girls were playing in a corner of the room, and whenever the sound of their laughter would break out, Eben Austin would frown. Nancy Austin beckoned to Jared as he came into the room.

"Hurry, boy, and do somewhat to keep your sisters quiet. Can't you see how it angers your father when they laugh?"

Jared nodded and waved a finger at Thankful, the elder of the two girls. She came across the room swiftly and threw herself against her half-brother, eager to prattle to him. Jared put his finger to his lips and her babble ceased. She looked at him questioningly. Mary came more slowly. Jared drew them both down beside him at one end of the long hearth; then he brushed a tile clean and took a cinder from the fire.

" 'Tis a special kind of cinder," he whispered.

"Can it make pictures?" Thankful whispered back.

"Yes, but only if everyone is quiet. If we say a word, the cinder will stop making pictures and jump back into the fire. It fears easily and likes the warm ash."

"Shall we tell Father and the stranger to cease their talk?" Thankful asked.

"No, no; it only minds talk close by."

The sisters watched Jared draw one picture after another on the tile, his way of telling a story. There was quiet in the room save for the voices of the men and the light steps of Nancy Austin on the bare floor as she laid the wooden plates on the table, filled the mugs with milk from the evening's milking, and took down from her cupboard a jar of spiced apples.

"I tell you, sir," the stranger was saying emphatically, "more and more people are coming to realize that walls of wood or plaster won't do–they're to be painted with scenes like those costly French wallpapers that are being imported or with designs as we stencilers are doing. It's the modern trend to bring beauty into our dwellings."

"We farming folk haven't time for such fol-de-rol, Mr. Toppan, or money either."

"That's where you make a mistake, sir. In the first place, it's hardly a matter of money since our custom is to do walls for our board and a little over; and in the second, ever since the war, people have had time to think about bringing beauty into their homes."

"The war is a long time past now," Eben Austin commented.

"Exactly," Mr. Toppan went on, "and we don't have to think any longer about defending ourselves or asserting our independence; we've proved one and achieved the other; so now we can give some time to the arts."

Nancy Austin ladled the stew from the big kettle onto the plates and called them all to supper. They drew up to the table and Eben gave a brief grace; then, as if uninterrupted, the two men went on with their talk. It was like a pendulum swinging between politics and art. They matched wits like flint and steel, and even when the conversation swung to discussion of crops and stock, the journeyman painter was as able to strike sparks as the farmer. Jared and the two little girls ate in silence, wide eyes on the guest, ears hearkening to the talk that was more wondrous than any tale in a book. Nancy Austin listened too, though it was not for her to comment.

When the babe in its cradle gave a fretful cry, she went back to the hearth, and, drawing up a low rocker, nursed the babe quietly. Then, as the men still lingered in their talk, Nancy motioned to the children to go upstairs to bed. The little girls were sleepy enough, but Jared—his eyes bright and a new intensity in his face—was loath to leave Mr. Toppan's presence.

Thankful and Mary were soon asleep under their patterned quilt, but there was no sleep for Jared. He pulled his quilt up to his shoulders, intently listening to the murmur of voices in the room below. His bed was near the chimney, and there was a crack between the floor and the bricks of the chimney. If only his father and the stranger would draw nearer the fire, he might be able to follow the wonderful meanderings of their talk.

Something about Mr. Toppan's presence in the house had touched his father so that the heavy frown across his brow had eased, and the tones of his voice were less grim as they mingled with the almost jaunty tones of the stranger. Jared thought he might even learn not to fear his father if Mr. Toppan stayed with them awhile. Jared knew that his father hated him and he knew why, but there was nothing he could do about it.

Eben Austin had come up to the New Hampshire land several years ago from his father's farm in Massachusetts. He had bought a parcel of rolling woodland, cleared the fields, and laid the foundation for his house. Then, with timber from his woods, his own strong arms, and the help of his neighbors, he had built his house. It was as true and sturdy a house as ever watched dawn come over the hills. In the cleared land before it, he had set out apple trees that would tide him through a season of small harvests, fill his own cellar, and give him enough to sell, for apples could be counted on to fetch a good price at all times. Two years more he had worked until his acres were fine and clean, yielding good harvest. The sturdy young apple trees had started to bear. Then he had gone back to his father's farm and for one whole summer—while his neighbors cared for his own land—he had courted lovely Lucy Lakin, daughter of a Boston merchant.

They were married in September and journeyed back together, over the rough roads, through the rich farming country of Massachusetts, and into the timbered wilderness of New Hampshire, where the farms were green clearings in a dense green land. Lucy's friends waved her farewell with mingled feelings when she rode off on the pillion seat behind tall, dark Eben Austin, for Lucy knew the grace of city ways, the charm of gentleness, and she seemed a strange one to brave the pioneer life. But Eben was strong, strong enough for them both, perhaps, and he was said to be a rich farmer in his own way, and they loved each other.

They reached their home in the mellow twilight of a September day. The fields were ruddy with harvest, apples hung red on the trees, wood stood piled by the door, and the neighbors had prepared such a feast to welcome them as filled Lucy's cupboard for many days. That autumn was long and warm, and the golden days moved with a bliss of their own well into December. Lucy took to the rugged life. Her hands that had done fine needlework and painted floral sprays on china found the same joy in the coarser work of spinning wheel and loom.

After Christmas, the winter came on hard and cruel. Snow lay deep in the fields and snow piled up over the windows of the one-story house. There were many mornings when Eben had to get up on the roof to clear drifted snow from the chimney before the fire could roar on the hearth. But Lucy was happy. There was a baby coming in the spring. During the long, quiet days when they were bound in by snow and Eben had only the animals in the barn to see to, she spun and wove and sang to herself while he fashioned a cradle out of smooth pine sheathing.

The winter hung on and the few days of warmth that came in April broke the cold but slightly. Lucy was longing to see the apple trees in blossom. Nothing else seemed to matter to her but that. With the first week of May, the sun shone steadily and the frost came out of the ground. The trees, so long held back, surged with sap, buds swelled and thickened, and within another week they were clouds of pink-and-white bloom.

Lucy and Eben stood in their doorway at sunset. Eben thought about the harvest of fruit such blossoms promised, and Lucy wondered whether she could give to the world in her blossoming such beauty as the trees had in theirs.

That night Lucy cried in sudden, bewildering pain. Their neighbor, Mrs. Thaxter, who had brought ten children of her own into the world and kept eight of them alive, was sent for at midnight. The baby came easily, quietly. He was a thin, small baby who had a fuzz of sandy down upon his head that looked like the shadow of his mother's fair hair, and nothing of his father's dark swarthiness. Lucy was blissful when they wrapped the boy in the garments she had woven for him and laid him on the pillow beside her.

"Welcome to you, little Jared," she said, then closed her eyes and slept.

The trees would blossom for only a week and Lucy did not want to lose a moment of it; so she sat by the window with the babe in her arms, feasting her eyes on white loveliness against a pale blue sky.

Jared was three days old when the grip of cold which the sun had failed to break came back. Such a bitter night settled down as would have been cold in January, and while the household slept, snow fell, inch after inch of it, tangling among the blossoms, piling up against the house. Lucy stirred and reached into the cradle, taking up the babe to cuddle against herself. As the night grew colder, she took a blanket from the bed to wrap the child in, then sheltered him with her body.

Eben was the first to see the havoc of the night, for the morning had made the world a tomb in which all hopes were buried. There would be no harvest from any blossoming tree this year, nor from any seed already sprouted and now frozen in the ground. Eben swore a dark oath; then, steeling himself against the bitter chill, he went to the hearth to rouse the coals. When the flames were roaring, he looked back toward the bed, but seeing Lucy still asleep with her arms nestling the babe, he moved quietly across the room and out to the barn to see to his animals.

An hour later he came back, his heart heavy within him and longing as he never had before for the comfort of Lucy's smile. Surprised that she was still abed, he stood beside her and called her name. A small hungry cry was the only answer. Lucy was dead, frozen in the pattern of sleep, but her body–still warm–had kept the child alive.

There had been no fruit that year, and though the apple trees blossomed every May, they bore no fruit again for many a year. Eben thought the child had put a curse upon them, and he hated his son with dark, relentless hatred.

Mrs. Thaxter came for Jared that morning and cared for the thin, small baby with the rest of her healthy brood. Eben Austin married again when Jared was nearly six, but this time he did not go away for a bride but went over the mountain to a neighboring settlement. Nancy Winship, the daughter of a farmer, was big-boned and rosy-cheeked, and her heart was full of kindness. She refused to marry Eben until Eben agreed to take his son back under his roof again. So the scrawny little boy of six trudged up the hill from the Thaxters', waving goodbye to small, plump Jennet, and came to live in the house where he was born.

Downstairs, the men had pushed back their chairs and were moving near the fire. Jared lay still, hoping to catch the trend of their talk, longing to hear more of the outside world which Mr. Toppan brought with him. Then Jared felt his ears pricking up like a dog's at a sharp sound, for they were talking about him.

"I tell you, sir, anyone who can draw like that should have a chance to learn more–why, it's a mighty clever bit of work for a cinder on a clay hearth tile!" Mr. Toppan's voice boomed pleasantly up the bricks of the fireplace and through the crack in the floor.

"That's the boy's doing," followed Eben's heavy voice. "He isn't good for anything but to dream and draw pictures. Mr. Toppan, if you knew–why, only last week he took the oxen down to the field to plow. . . ."

A hot blush of shame mounted Jared's cheeks as he heard his father tell of finding him with only two furrows broken in the field, and already it was near noontime. But the wild shadblow bush in blossom by the brook had been so beautiful that Jared had had to stop and draw it, using a piece of clay on a smooth gray boulder. He had not meant to take so long, and he would have finished the field by sundown. Jared longed to stop his ears as he heard his father's repetition of the tale, but he would not, for fear of missing Mr. Toppan's answer.

Eben Austin ceased with a harsh laugh. He did not tell Mr. Toppan that he had broken off the branch of blooming shad and beaten Jared with it until the boy lay sick and faint on the rough plowed land, weeping not from the hurt on his body, but at the frail white blossoms around him, dashed so rudely to the earth. Then the oxen had gone on under Eben's masterful hand, and the field had been plowed by evening.

There was a long silence, broken finally by Mr. Toppan's voice, deep and gentle. " 'Tis no sin to love beauty, but the boy is out of place here. I can use a keen apprentice. Let him journey with me tomorrow."

Another long silence, then Eben's words–reluctant, slow, not saying yes, not saying no. "There's times in the year–planting and harvest–when we need every pair of hands, even those of the smallest children."

"I'll pay you the wages of an apprentice. You could hire a strong lad for those times."

"What are the wages?" Eben asked, yielding with difficulty.

"Naught but keep the first year while he's learning; fifty cents a week afterward for five years; then he'll command his own wages."

" 'Tis done," Eben said, "but there's no help if he brings as much bad luck to you as he has to me."

If there were more words, Jared did not hear them, because of the light sound of Nancy Austin's footsteps coming up the stairs to the loft.

"Are you awake, Jared?" she asked in a low voice.

"Yes"–he reached out his hand in the dark and drew her to the bed–"and I've heard what my father and the stranger have been saying."

"Then you must call him stranger no longer, since he's to be your master."

There was silence in the room.

"Are you glad, boy?" Nancy asked kindly.

"The gladness makes the words stop within me," Jared said, and he squeezed her hand tightly. "I'll be a great painter one day, Mother Nancy; then I'll come back to you."

"Don't have fancy notions about yourself, Jared," she said sharply. "Learn to be a good workman and leave it at that." She bent over and kissed him; then she smoothed the quilt on the little girls' bed, and soon her step could be heard going down the stairs.

A wave of happiness swept over Jared in the dark of the loft, and because the waking was so longed for, sleep came easily to him.

The next morning Jared was about his chores early, stacking wood on the hearth and bringing in the fresh milk. Driving the cows to pasture, he left them near the brook, then splashed barefoot through its waters and over the field to the Thaxter house.

"Mama Thaxter," he cried, rushing into the house, "I'm going off with Mr. Toppan to learn to be a painter!"

Mother Thaxter put down the long iron spoon with which she was stirring porridge on the hob and caught Jared in her wide arms. He had been like one of her own for six years, and her heart had ached often since he had left her–ached because she had not been able to put flesh on his bones as she had with her own children, ached because there seemed so little chance of his ever being happy, living in the dark shadow of his father's hatred.

"Sit down, boy, with a plate of porridge and some good rich milk, and tell me about it."

Jared would have rather talked than eaten, but Mother Thaxter would not listen to him until he had spooned up half the plateful, and then she kept a watchful eye that he eat the remainder. Jared spoke eagerly, telling all he knew.

"And in five years, Mama Thaxter, I'll be my own master. Then I'll come back and paint all the walls of your house!" Jared put back his head and laughed with the joy of it, for even saying such words gave him the feel of a brush between his fingers and made him seem a man in his own right.

She smiled at him, happy at last for him.

"I must go, Mama Thaxter," Jared said suddenly. "It would not do for me to anger my father this morning."

She put a kiss on his upturned face and held him close to her. "God bless you, little Jared; you'll be a man when you come back to me, and may you be as strong in body as you are now in heart."

Jared ran out of the house. Jennet was coming back from the barn where she had been feeding the chickens, still holding her apron up, so that the corn she had left might not be wasted. The wind was tossing her hair about. The blue of her dress was like the blue of the sky. Jared stood still and watched her as she came toward him–such a firm step, such strong arms, and eyes that had the light of the morning dancing in them.

"I'm going away with Mr. Toppan–the journeyman painter–I'm an apprentice now," Jared said proudly.

"When will you be back?" she asked.

"In five years. I'll be a man then."

"Oh!" Jennet exclaimed. He might have said forever, for five years seemed that long.

"Good-bye." Jared turned and started across the field.

"Good-bye." Her voice came after him on the light wind.

"I'll come back for you, Jennet," he called to her.

At the top of the hill he turned and looked back. She was still standing there. He waved, thinking he would always remember her like that–a brave, strong girl with the frolicsome winds of April whipping about her and a dress the color of the sky.

The Austin family members were talking of Jared's going as they sat at breakfast. Thankful was crying. Mary, too young to know what was happening, turned her wide dark eyes on everyone in turn.

"Make yourself ready," Eben Austin said as Jared entered the room, "for Mr. Toppan will be leaving soon."

With Nancy's help, Jared was soon ready to go on his journeying. He had only one pair of shoes, and he wore those on Sundays when they went to meeting; and he had only one suit, which Nancy had made long in the legs and arms for him to grow into. Nancy smoothed the rough homespun cloth and fastened a button here and there. Then she took him in her arms and kissed him.

"You'll be too big for me to kiss when you come back," she said, trying to smile.

Jared shook his head, wondering why all the words he longed to say had left him. He turned quickly and ran out to the barn. It was cool and friendly there. The smell of hay was good, and even better was the gentle whinnying and mooing of the creatures who knew him well. Jared picked up Mr. Toppan's saddle and started to prepare the mare for her journey, wondering how he would be able to walk fast enough to keep pace with her long stride.

A shadow came across the sunlight that flooded in the barn door. Jared turned to see Eben Austin with a saddle over his arm, a small saddle, quite new, and one that Jared had not seen before.

"Is the mare ready?"

"Yes, Father."

"The gray filly is down in the lower field. Put this saddle on her."

Jared held out his hands for the saddle. "For me?" he asked.

Eben nodded. "The bridle too. I made this saddle for your mother. It's small, but you'll never be a big one, and 'till do for you."

Jared looked up into his father's eyes. It was the first time Eben had mentioned his mother, and to the boy it seemed as if a wall had broken down between them.

"Thank you," Jared said. Then, with the saddle over one arm and the light bridle over the other, he raced down to the lower field.

Chapter Two

Jared, riding off beside Mr. Toppan on that April morning of 1810, did not know what to expect of the new life before him. He had held the bridle of Mr. Toppan's mare and noticed how carefully the big man threw his leg over the saddle with its bag of brushes and paints; then he had flung his thin leg over the Gray One's back and settled himself into the saddle that still creaked from newness. Mr. Toppan had doffed his wide-brimmed hat and Jared had waved to Eben and Nancy standing on the doorstone, to Thankful and Mary clinging to Nancy's skirts, and to the babe in her arms. Then they had turned their horses' heads toward the road and started off.

In a last glance, Jared saw the twisted shapes of the apple trees before the house; over the hill he saw the thin spiral of smoke from the Thaxter's chimney. Those things were home, and his heart felt a pang of longing at leaving them; but he had learned early to steel himself against bodily pain, and that of the heart was little different. So he turned his eyes to the road ahead and to the uneven line of the mountains that rose up against the sky.

Always the mountains had bound his world–the distant blue ones to the north, the pyramid-shaped one that reared itself high in lonely splendor to the west, and the tapering line to the east that rose up from near their own land. When he was a little boy, he had thought that the mountains rimmed the world and beyond them there was nothing else. Later, when he had had a few months of school, he learned that the rest of the world lay beyond the mountains–some of it evil, some of it good.

Mr. Toppan and Jared rode through the pass over the mountains. When they stood still for a moment on the crest to rest their horses, Jared could see both the road behind them reaching back into the known world and the road ahead. The wind whistled through the gap, and he shivered.

"Are you afeard, boy?" Mr. Toppan asked kindly. "Are you wanting to turn back?"

Jared felt the pull of the road they had traveled over and all the known things it led back to: Mother Thaxter's warm kitchen and Jennet in her blue dress, Nancy's kindness and her attempts to make up for Eben's anger, the little girls and the baby; then the long years of planting and harvesting, wintering and planting again, and a boy growing to be a farmer like his father, looking out to the mountains and always wondering what lay beyond them.

"No, Mr. Toppan, I'm not fearful. Just full of wondering. I like the looks of the road ahead."

"So be it then." Mr. Toppan pressed his mare forward and the Gray One drew into her stride obediently. "But mark you, boy, since you have chosen one road, follow it with your whole heart. From this time forth we speak no more of the farms on the back side of the mountain. The Lord did not give me a good pair of eyes for nothing and with but one of them I could see well enough what your life has been–and what it can be. You've a gift in your fingers which God can use, but lay yourself open for the work and think of the past only when that quietness comes which can smooth the sharp edges of memory."

"Yes, Mr. Toppan." Jared found it easier to say that now they were going down the other side of the mountain.

"For five years you'll be my apprentice," Mr. Toppan went on, "and five years from the 12th day of April 1810, you can mount this same road and return to your people. You'll be your own master then, and no man can lift a hand to you, save to pay you well for your services."

"What if I would work for you more than five years, Mr. Toppan?"

"Five years is long enough for any man to serve another when he has the gift I think you have."

They rode on in silence. The sun climbed high in the sky, and its warmth was lavish on the earth. Warblers sang in the trees edging the road, and a brook recently loosed from winter's lock of ice and snow raced over boulders in its course to the valley. Often a deer sprang across the path before them, and more than once the underbrush moved heavily where a bear, padding along and sniffing the ground, had stepped aside to let them pass.

"A journeyman painter's life is not an easy one, Jared," Mr. Toppan was saying. "We're here one week and there another. Sometimes we get no pay but our board, and sometimes we get no thanks. But it's a good life, too."

"It must be a fine thing to use those big brushes that you have in your saddlebag," Jared commented.

"You shall see soon enough, for we've a room to do at an inn ahead of us on the road. If the Gray One can do her thirty miles as well as my mare, we'll be there by nightfall and at work in the morning."

Jared, stumbling for words in his joy, found only an apology. "But, Mr. Toppan, I've never used a brush."

"I can teach you, boy, and learning comes best by doing."

They had been traveling three hours or more, sometimes in silence, sometimes in talk, when Mr. Toppan reined in his horse by a ford. There was a clearing and some fallen logs to sit on, new greening grass for the horses to graze, and the brook for them all to drink from.

"We won't be the first travelers to stop here for our luncheon," Mr. Toppan commented as he slipped the bridle from his horse. Then he stretched his booted legs out on the ground with his back against a beech tree. Its smooth bark was a bulletin board of initials carved intricately and laboriously while other horses had been grazing and other travelers resting.

The brown mare stepped into the brook and drank deeply of the water. Jared, still keeping his hand on the Gray One's reins, let her water beside the mare; then he led her over to the grassy spot.

"She's a young thing still, Mr. Toppan, and I'll not let her loose this first day," Jared explained; " 'twould do me no good if she took a fancy into her head to go back over the mountains to her own pasture."

Mr. Toppan smiled. "That's right, Jared; keep a good eye on your horse, for a horse is a journeyman's partner in business." He took from his pocket a package of bread and cheese which Nancy Austin had given him that morning.

Jared secured the Gray One to a log and went upstream, above where the horses had been drinking, to get fresh water in a flat bottle Mr. Toppan carried in his pack. Returning, he sat on the fallen log near Mr. Toppan. Breaking bread together, drinking cold forest-drawn water out of the same bottle, with two horses cropping grass nearby and birds singing in the sweet April air, made Jared feel that the windows of heaven had opened to him.

"Has the brown mare been your partner long, Mr. Toppan?" he asked.

"Yes, for many a long year we've gone seeking work together," he answered, "and she's done more for me than my brushes have." Mr. Toppan looked at Jared. "Bless you, boy; you haven't lived as much as half the time I've been traveling, yet how the world has changed! When I first took to the road, I was willing enough to do any job that came my way–a piece of carpentering here or painting there with my board as my wage. In those days there wasn't time or inclination for aught but needed things."

"Was the traveling hard then?"

Mr. Toppan nodded. "The roads through the forests were mere trails, and sometimes you had to hold your eyes close to the slashes on the trees to keep from straying. Many of the farms were just clearings with the stumps still standing in the fields, and there were more log cabins than houses. A man like me carried a gun as well as a pack then."

"Did you meet with the Indians often?"

"No," Mr. Toppan said with a shake of his head. "Bears and wolverines were the most troublesome, but I stayed in many a cabin with old folk who had tales to tell of the Indians–of homes burned to the ground and women and children carried off to be sold to the French in Canada. But that's all a story of the past, and so is the war which gave us the liberty we've yet to show we can use well." He sighed. "It's so far behind us that it looks as if we might have to fight another war, on the sea this time."

"What is it all for, Mr. Toppan?"

"I'm not the best to explain, boy, but when you win one battle you often have to prove you knew what you were fighting for and win the next. I've been in the north country all winter and have heard little enough news. Tonight at the inn we'll fill our ears right enough."

Jared's tongue was trembling with questions he longed to ask, but Mr. Toppan had closed his eyes and folded his hands over his broad chest. Jared reined the Gray One near him and stroked her soft nose.

All around them was the forest–tall trees breaking into new foliage, silent depths which never man had trod, which knew no sound save the stealthy feet of Indians and the quick flight of wild things. But it was the same forest that man was pushing back, making clearings in, raising homes. And after the work had gone well, he sought to bring beauty into those homes, taking his patterns from the careless tracery in nature and, with infinite care, reproducing them.

Thinking back, as Mr. Toppan had said he could do in quietness, to the home beyond the mountains, Jared saw the rough edges blurred with happiness. There was his father giving him the Gray One; Nancy Austin, with her eyes shining like stars out of the darkness of the loft, telling him of his apprenticeship; Jennet coming back from feeding the chickens, the April wind tossing her hair. A few days ago, Jared had come upon a spring bubbling in a field, the water reaching up from the earth and tumbling onward in a cool stream. The natural joy at the heart of all creation was like that spring, he thought, bubbling from dark depths and, once released, impatient to water the earth.

The brown mare had been standing at rest with sagging head and drooping tail. Now, as if at a signal, she raised her head, stiffened her tail, and moved a pace or two until she could push her nose against her master's face. Mr. Toppan stirred and opened his eyes.

"All right, girl," he said drowsily. He sat up and, seeing Jared sitting opposite him, explained, "She never lets me sleep more than an hour when we are on our way."

They had soon tightened their saddle girths and mounted, riding on through the green stillness. Every mile was like the last, for the woods did not terminate, and the road was rutted and rocky.

By midafternoon they had come into a different countryside, and the forest hung behind them like a curtain of green let down over the world. They were in Massachusetts now, and the road had widened so that two carts could have passed each other in safety. There were meadows and pastures surrounding them, and rich fields where the earth had been newly broken by the plow and was being planted. They passed a farmhouse every few miles, with sheep and cattle in the pastures and horses working the fields–such a sight to Jared after the great lumbering oxen Eben Austin had worked his land with. They passed more people on the road, sometimes overtaking a cart heavily laden with farm produce seeking its slow way to market; sometimes joining a fellow journeyman with whom they would ride for a while, exchanging news. Mr. Toppan waved to a tin peddler resting his horse by the roadside, and the brief greeting was capped by the phrase, "I'll see you at Cinnamon John's tonight."

"Do you know everyone in the world, Mr. Toppan?" Jared asked, marveling at the greetings given along the way.

Mr. Toppan laughed. "Not a mite of them, boy, but we often meet on the road, and some of us will be sitting around Cinnamon John's table tonight."

"Is that the inn where we've a room to do?"

"It is, and everyone calls its keeper Cinnamon John."

"Why, Mr. Toppan?"

"Why–because he sailed on one of the first ships that went to the Indies, and no one in these parts had ever tasted cinnamon until John brought some back with him."

It was near dusk when they approached the inn. It stood at a crossroads with an ample barn close to the road and beside the inn, a trough where travelers could water their horses and splash some of the dust of the road off their own hands and faces. Mr. Toppan reined up at the door and was greeted with a hearty halloo from within. Then the door was opened and Cinnamon John came out. He was a thickset, grizzly man with a smile as broad as his well-filled paunch.

"Toppan, I've been looking for you for a month," he called out.

"John, I said I'd be here when the snow was off the roads."

"Snow!" John roared. "We've not seen a flick of it here for six weeks."

"I've come down from the north country, and it's but recently cleared off up there."

Mr. Toppan dismounted by the door and Cinnamon John clapped him on the shoulders. Jared slid off the Gray One and held the reins of both horses. Cinnamon John cocked an eye at him.

"Who's the lad?" he asked.

"My apprentice, John," Mr. Toppan answered with a note of pride in his voice. "And we'll start on your job tomorrow if you've got some milk set for me."

"Oh, there's always milk enough," John said, "but don't they feed the children any better in the north?" His eye ran over Jared's bony body. "Always heard the land was poorly, but he's the runtiest bit of boy I've ever seen."

"He's a good one," Mr. Toppan said with a laugh. Then he turned to Jared. "Put the horses in the barn, boy, and come in when you've settled them."

The two men disappeared into the inn, and Jared led the horses to the barn. There were bedded stalls waiting. He unsaddled the mares and rubbed them down well with hand-fuls of hay; then he threw blankets over them. They had gone well–the brown mare because she knew her job, the gray because she was young and high-spirited; but they were both tired and drooped their heads wearily into their mangers. Jared set the saddles carefully against the wall. Going from the barn to the inn, he stopped at the trough to splash himself clean with the cold water.

The lights of the inn gleamed out warmly against the approach of night. There were a clatter of dishes and savory smells coming from the kitchen, and fragrant smoke billowed out of the huge chimney. Other travelers were arriving in carriages, on foot, on horseback, leading their tired animals into the barn, then opening the door of the inn and disappearing into the light and warmth within.

Jared stood by the trough, quivering with happiness. He wanted to watch the door of the inn open and shut many times. He wanted to go on thinking of the wonders that lay across its threshold, for he knew that his first step into that world beyond the door would be his first step into manhood. He squared his shoulders. Holding his head high, he went toward that wide and welcoming door.

Inside, there was a hubbub of voices, the flickering of candlelight, the movement of shadows on the walls, the enticing smell of good food ready to be served. There was a fire on the wide hearth and black kettles simmering over it; on the table a roast stood ready to be carved. One long table ran the length of the room, its bare surface shining with the gleam of pewter plates and tankards. Benches ranged on either side of the table, each with room for a dozen or more people. At a word from Cinnamon John, the men moved toward their places, and Jared slipped in among them beside Mr. Toppan. The benches were drawn up, and Cinnamon John sank his carving knife into the roast.

It was good, that dinner, and the men ate heartily. When the empty platter that had held the roast was removed, Cinnamon John's wife opened the door of the brick oven and brought out a pudding browned to perfection, with an aroma all its own rising from it in tantalizing, invisible spirals. Jared did not need to ask any questions, though he had never met such a fragrance before. This was the spice that had made the inn famous up and down the countryside.

Talk that was loud and free and jovial resounded in the room, but it was not until people had been fed, the table cleared, and the dishes removed for washing that the men gave themselves to talk in earnest. Most of the travelers had been wintering or working in the North and were starved for news of the world. Cinnamon John had some to share, and a tinker, newly arrived from Boston, had the most to give.

James Madison had rounded out his first year of the presidency with little distinction. He was desirous, as Jefferson had been before him, to keep peace, and by the diplomatic means at his disposal he had, so far, kept trade open with Great Britain. But Napoleon was rapidly making matters worse by seizing all the American vessels he could lay hold on.

"A trap it is to embroil us with England," Cinnamon John exclaimed angrily, while a murmur of assent rolled over the group.

"When Bonaparte is finally imprisoned and the world at peace," Mr. Toppan interjected, "what, I ask you, will the papers fill their columns with?"

"Aye, that's a question," the tinker reflected. Talk or write as one would these days, the main hinge was always Napoleon Bonaparte.

So much for foreign affairs, but those at home were curiously influenced by those abroad. It was difficult to talk of one without coming back to the other. The Northwest was opening swiftly, and already New England men were being tempted from their stubborn land. There was rich soil awaiting them in new states being carved from territory that had been lately acquired from the Indians, sometimes honorably, sometimes shamefully, and often through open warfare.

In spite of rocks and shallows, the tide of emigration which would mark the first half of the century had already begun to flow, and the face of New England was changing. Where farms had been, factories were springing up. Clocks, chairs, textiles, and notions of all kinds were being manufactured, and peddlers were carrying them into the South and the West.

The young country, as the knowledgeable tinker from Boston went on to explain, was like a nut in a cracker, with clashes on the high seas making one pinch, and clashes on the frontier the other, both branching from the same stem. Jefferson might have extricated the meat of the nut without having it broken when the shell was crushed, but could Madison? That was the question asked by many.

Jared listened until his head nodded with sleep, and Mr. Toppan suddenly remembered that a young boy should have been sent to the loft hours ago.

"The coming industry can't harm our trade," he commented as he watched Jared slowly mounting the stairs, "but 'twill tend to heighten it."

The next morning early, the various travelers who had stopped overnight began to take their leave. There was a tramping of booted feet on the kitchen floor, the sound of voices, and the clinking of coins, as payment was made to Cinnamon John–sometimes in cash, more often in other things. Money was scarce in those days, and an innkeeper was glad to settle accounts with a bushel of apples or sack of wool, some labor, a few needed notions from a peddler, or heavier stuff from a team going to the markets. There was a stamping and neighing in the barn as horses were saddled or harnessed, and a calling back and forth as men got under way.

By seven o'clock only Mr. Toppan and Jared were left at the long table by the deep fireplace, and Mr. Toppan had pushed his plate away and was beginning to make rough sketches on a piece of paper.

"Jared, did you see to the horses?"

"Yes, Mr. Toppan. I fed and watered them an hour ago."

"And my saddlebags?"

"I'll fetch them." Jared darted from the room.

When he returned with the bags and their precious freight of brushes and paint powders, Cinnamon John and Mr. Toppan were deep in a discussion of the designs for the large room on the second floor of the inn, the length of which ran across the entire front of the house. Although there were fireplaces at either end and windows well spaced, the walls of the room were bare, and the grayish white plaster had a ghostly look.

Cinnamon John stood in the center of the room. "It should be the brightest room in the house, a place where I can gather all my friends together. But it looks like the inside of a tomb. What can you do to it, Toppan?"

Mr. Toppan looked at the innkeeper. "John, what means most to you in this life?" he asked. "Mind, I'm not asking you to mention your wife or your family, or that powerful stallion you've got in the barn, or the porker you're fattening; but what do you like to remember?"

John scratched his grizzled head, then he said slowly, "I like to remember the East–the spicy smell of it, the sun shining on the dark skins of the people, the birds with their fancy plumes, and the odd fruit hanging on the trees. I'm a land-locked sailor, Toppan, and I've got an inn instead of a ship, but if I could have one wish, it would be to sail around the Horn again before I die." He laughed his loud, roistering laugh. "But man, that's got naught to do with these white walls!"

Mr. Toppan nodded his head slowly. "John, d'you trust me? Will you let me go my way on these walls, and will you keep below until I'm finished?"

John narrowed his eyes. "I wouldn't do it with anyone else in the world, but I will with you, Toppan." He turned on his heel and started toward the door; then he looked back for a moment. "While you're here, the best that Cinnamon John has to give will be yours, and if I can't put some flesh on that scrawny runt I've no business to be keeping an inn."

Mr. Toppan smiled and an embarrassed smile broke over Jared's face.

"There are firkins of milk in the shed for you," Cinnamon John said. "How long do you plan to be doing the room?"

"A month or more, John."

"Then I'll turn your horses out to pasture, and remember"–he wagged one of his thick, round fingers at Mr. Toppan–"if I like your work you'll have twenty silver dollars!" He turned and left the room.

Jared faced Mr. Toppan. "And if he doesn't like it?"

"We'll have no more than our board," Mr. Toppan said shortly, "but none of that now, for I don't begin a job thinking it won't be liked. Know your man, Jared Austin, before you undertake his work, and you'll do it so it will please him."

They were the first words of many that the master was to say to his apprentice, and Jared would remember them always.

Now things began to happen quickly as Jared worked with Mr. Toppan. A wide plank was set on trestles to serve as a table. The saddlebags were unpacked and their precious contents stood forth–a series of brushes of varying shapes and sizes; several packets containing dry colors: green, ocher, blue, brown, yellow, venetian red. There were measuring tools, a cord, and some chalk. There were blocks of wood with designs stamped on them and sheets of heavy paper–some plain, some with designs already cut out on them.

An exclamation of joy came from Jared as he saw the stencils, for they were what he had been striving for when he had cut a clumsy design on the leaf.

"Now, boy, fetch the milk from the buttery and two or three wooden buckets that are hanging there for us. Then all will be in readiness."

When Jared returned with the firkins of nicely soured milk and later with the empty buckets, Mr. Toppan was standing in the middle of the room, looking at the walls. A smile was stealing over his face, and Jared knew that Mr. Toppan was not seeing the bare walls but the decorated ones. Jared felt then that perhaps his first lesson as an apprentice was to learn not to ask questions, but to wait, and when his master spoke, to listen. So he tucked his legs under him on the bench running along the wall and waited, wondering if–after he had been with Mr. Toppan for a while–he, too, would see the finished work before a brush had been so much as lifted or a stencil held to the wall. Often he had tried to make what he was dimly seeing in his mind come before his eyes, with a cinder on the hearth, or with a leaf upon a stone. Now he began to see that it must be clear in his own mind first before he attempted to fashion it; then it would find its imprint quickly through whatever medium he chose.

Mr. Toppan went over to the firkins of milk. He put his finger into the firming mass and tasted it, then nodded. "It's soured to the turn we want," he said.

Taking a packet of ocher powder, he poured its contents into the milk, mixing it round and round with a wooden ladle.

It looked as if the burning amber of a sunset had been scooped into a wooden bucket.

"It's strong, lad, but when it dries on the wall it will be the color we want. Always mix your washes darker than you want them, for they dry that much lighter."

He took the widest and flattest of his brushes, dipped it carefully into the bucket, and showed Jared how the color was to be washed on the walls.

"Am I to do that, Mr. Toppan?" Jared asked, scarcely believing that such a trust was his.

Mr. Toppan nodded. "Go lightly, evenly. You may be at it all day while I'm busy at the stencils."

There were a few further instructions which to Jared seemed like a song set to the music in his heart; then he dipped the brush and climbed up the small ladder to the ceiling and began sweeping the color down to the floor in clean, even strokes. The walls looked far too vivid for beauty when they were wet, but as the wash dried, the color softened. Jared gazed with pleasure at the warmth with which the room had begun to glow.

Mr. Toppan, meanwhile, worked at cutting his stencils. On stiff paper he first traced his design, then, taking a sharp knife–which was constantly being resharpened on a small whetstone–he cut the stencils out. Often the edges of the pattern were beveled so that they would lie with perfect smoothness when applied to the walls, and so provide a sharp outline to the design. Intricate and many were the stencils that lay cut and ready for use.

Jared longed to watch Mr. Toppan cutting; but though few words had been exchanged between them, he knew that his job was to apply the background color for the stencils. If he did that well, someday he would be taught how to cut stencils with a knife as sharp and shiny as Mr. Toppan's own.

"It's a simple tool," Mr. Toppan said once, holding a stencil up to the light to see it more clearly, "but it's served the world well through many ages. And there's nothing fancy about it, for stenciling is as homespun a craft as weaving. Take what you know, the way a woman takes the wool from her sheep and spins it for her loom; take the colors God has given us in earth and sky and flowering things; then use the good sense that's your heritage."

"Will it always be beautiful, Mr. Toppan?"

"Yes," he answered with conviction, "if you keep true to your own feeling for beauty. Some may call it dainty, some may call it daring–but none will call it aught but beautiful."

"What do you mean by keeping true?" Jared asked, laying down his brush to rest his arm.

Mr. Toppan looked at him until his eyes seemed not to see the boy Jared, but the man Jared might become, then he said quietly, "It's letting God have your life, so that your hands do the work He wants you to do. You've begun rightly, Jared, for that's the beginning and end of all my teaching."

They worked until dusk. The buckets of paint were empty. Jared's arm ached from its day-long drawing of the brush from ceiling to floor. He laid the brush down, his fingers trembling as his arm hung limp at his side. Mr. Toppan smiled at the pile of cut stencils. The room was darkening quickly, but it was darkening in shades of gold–colors of the sunset still warm, though light had gone.

Mr. Toppan nodded his head. "It's good," he said.

He scanned the ceiling, but not a brush stroke marred the plaster. His eyes swept the floor but found no splash of paint or careless drop to fasten on.

"In fact, it's well done," he said slowly. "Perhaps I made a good choice when I hired you from your father. Yes?"

Jared was too tired to do anything but smile, and the room was too dark by then to reveal the full meaning of his smile.

Chapter Three

The room in Cinnamon John's inn was done.

Mr. Toppan and his apprentice had worked day after day, and no one had asked them any questions. Sour milk had been supplied for their paints, and from peddlers fresh from the cities, Mr. Toppan had bought packets of dry colors to replenish his dwindling store. They had begun their work when the day was young and finished it when sunset filtered through the wide west windows; then they had gone down to the kitchen to sit at the long table and eat and talk with the other travelers. Most apprentices were relegated to the hearth with a bowl of scalded milk or bean porridge and a brown crust, but Jared had been privileged from the start, sitting at the same table with the men and sharing the same fare.

After supper Mr. Toppan would linger by the fire; it was a time when conversation that somehow patched together the ends of the earth was exchanged. To sit by the hearth of an inn those days was to have an ear to the world, for there was not a passing traveler without some whit of news. Jared would more often climb the stairs to the loft, and, pulling the quilt up over his shoulders, snuggle down to sleep in its folds. The sense of happiness that pervaded him made him feel warm and secure. Beauty was taking shape under his hands and before his eyes; at last he could be a part of all the beauty that God had given to the world–the lilacs coming into their darkly purple and deeply scented bloom; the majesty and music of words he heard read from the Bible when he went to meeting on Sunday. On that day alone out of the whole week, and for all the hours of it, the journeyman painter and his apprentice laid down their brushes.

As they worked together day after day, Jared learned how the work was done. Sometimes he was clumsy; sometimes he made mistakes which took a long time for their undoing; but through it all he felt a skill coming into his fingers. Now the stencil never slipped under his hand, for he knew how to hold it; now he never loaded too much paint on his brushes, for he knew how to dip them; now he never mixed shades amiss, for he knew the right proportions for the colors they were using.

After the walls had been washed with solid color and the stencils cut, they had worked for the next few days with cord and chalk, spacing the designs, marking on the walls where each one would go. When that had been done, they stood in the center of the room and saw how the finished walls would look.

"Art, Jared," Mr. Toppan said then, "is to do just enough to satisfy, just enough to intrigue. The spacing of your stencil reveals your skill more than anything else you do. Crowd your designs, and you have bound the wings of fantasy; space them well, and you give it full flight."

Jared nodded. He could understand that. It explained why, when he lay on his back by his father's brook and looked up at the sky, he saw more beauty in the budding branches of early spring than in the leafy foliage of summer. It was the beauty of space; and space–as Mr. Toppan said–gave freedom to thought.

"But the frieze just below the ceiling, now that is different," Mr. Toppan went on. "For we must hold the design in a frame as it were; so we depend upon the frieze to do that. We must also frame the view from each window, and there again our frieze will do it. But within the frieze, that's where space counts."

Jared had held one end of the cord while Mr. Toppan had taken the measuring line and the chalk. Carefully he made his indications where each stencil should lie, so that its relationship with every other one in the room would be balanced and serene.

Jared's fingers began to itch for the brushes; so long a time it seemed they were working with intangible things; so long a time the room was no more than yellow walls with chalk dots. But Mr. Toppan saw the walls as if they were done.

"Sir, when shall we really start to work?" Jared asked hungrily, after nearly a week had gone by.

"Work?" Mr. Toppan looked surprised. "But what do you think we have been doing?"

"Getting things ready."

Mr. Toppan gazed at Jared and his eyes, warm as they were, had something to them that seemed to go through the boy's thin body. "Getting ready is the biggest part of any job, and the hardest, Jared," he answered slowly. "Have you never seen a house a-building–the foundation first, the heavy frame, the ridgepole, and all the thought beforehand? These are the things you do not see when it is finished, but you'd have no house without them. Lay your foundation true and firm, my boy, prepare your work well; the rest all but does itself."

Jared said nothing more. He felt rebuked, not by Mr. Toppan's words but by his own brashness. He must learn to wait–among all else that he was learning–to lay the groundwork like a true master, to seek beauty through the eye of his mind instead of turning to the fortuitous skill of his fingers. When, in patience and humility, he saw that beauty dwelt secure, he could be confident that it would reproduce itself and by its own force. Fingers and brush would be the mediums then, not the prime actors.

"Now, lad, we'll mix our colors."

Mr. Toppan moved over to the makeshift table and opened the different packets of dry powders, pouring them into earthen jars with glazed interiors; then he added to them the right amount of soured milk to give a pliant mixture.

"There's a secret with colors," he explained. "If you want to make people happy just by the seeing of them, use colors that have kinship with each other. People won't always know it's your colors. They'll think they just happen to feel happy; but that doesn't matter." He swung around from his mixing and looked out the window. "There's not an artist since the beginning of the world that hasn't had the same teacher—nature; for there's not a day in the year but that the purest beauty anyone can see is in the world that God made. Look there now, Jared, and tell me what colors you see."

Jared moved nearer the window. It was open and a breeze fragrant with springtime blew in on him. His eyes rested on the green pasture where two colts were frolicking, then on a nearby meadow where the green was mottled with the bright yellow of dandelions, then on across brown tree trunks and newly turned earth to the blue haze of distant hills, melting into the azure reaches of the sky.

"Green, Mr. Toppan," Jared said, "and gold, blue, and brown, and perhaps a sort of color like bricks before they are kilned."

"Ocher, we'll call that last," Mr. Toppan added. "Good enough, Jared, and those colors bear kinship with each other. Mix any two together and you'll get another one. Now, try again. If you were looking eastward across those hills and it were early dawn, what colors would you see heralding the sun?"

"In winter or in summer, sir?"

"Both. Tell me winter first."

Jared half-closed his eyes to see the flow of dawn over the mountains near his home, to see it as he had so often seen it, shivering in the cold winds of January.

"White in the east, then lifting into silver," Jared began, "then warmed as the silver turns to gold. Suddenly the sun itself, like a golden wave, splashes over the world."

"Now, summer?"

"Oh," Jared said, breathing deeply, and the memory of the warmth of a summer dawn made his lean body shed its tenseness. "Here we begin with gold. The gold turns into orange, then crimson. The sky glows with scarlet and the earth looks warm and rich. Then such a globe of fire comes over the mountains as makes the corn in the fields draw some of the color into its cobs, and the fruits on the trees borrow a tinge."

Mr. Toppan slapped his hands on his knees and laughed heartily. "That's right, Jared, and we could go on and on. Think of your flamboyant trees in autumn, the subtle blending of a cock pheasant's plumage, the pattern of the sky repeated on a bluebird's breast. We'll take our cue from nature, holding well to the colors that hold well with each other."

They mixed their paints and the next day commenced their work. Mr. Toppan did most of it, the different friezes and all the intricate designs. Jared held the paint pots, cleaned the brushes, and rubbed the stencil edges free of hardened paint. When Mr. Toppan needed both hands, Jared held the stencil firmly to the wall and watched the deft moves of the brush as the design was filled in. With some patterns, one stencil was laid upon another for the overlaying of color. Their progress was slow, for Mr. Toppan was a careful craftsman, made doubly so by experience, placing his patterns precisely, and laying his paint wisely.

After many days, Mr. Toppan turned the stencils and the brushes over to Jared, leaving the bit of wall behind the door for him to do. Jared was happy, and his heart beat so hard and fast that he could hear nothing else. He held the stencil firmly as he had held it so many days for Mr. Toppan, but try as he would, he could not keep his hands from trembling. The stencil slipped off its line, and an ugly smudge of paint marred the lacy clarity of the pattern.

"Oh, sir, see what I have done!" Jared cried out, and his voice broke with chagrin and disappointment.

Mr. Toppan crossed the room and stood by Jared. Jared raised his arm to shield his head from the blow he dreaded. There was silence for a moment, and a robin singing outside in an apple tree seemed to Jared like a cry of pain, for his world had darkened so. Then Mr. Toppan's hand closed firmly around Jared's wrist, and he moved the bowed arm until it hung straight and stiff at the boy's side.

"Stand like a man, Jared, and face another like an equal. So, the stencil slipped? You've held it firm enough for me for days past."

"My fingers were trembling, sir. I couldn't hold the stencil still."

"Don't blame your fingers; it was not they who trembled first, was it?" he asked kindly. "Come, Jared, you're man enough to face your work and do it. Take the stencil and lay it for the pattern next in line, straight and true. You can do it."

Jared picked up the stencil and held it to the wall. He dipped his brush and poised it for a moment over the space. A calm had come over him and with it a feeling of power, as he rose to do what Mr. Toppan expected him to do.

Mr. Toppan stood by him until every curving line of the pattern had been filled in and the stencil removed from the wall. The design was there, solid and simple, and as true as any other in the room.

"There's not a better one in the whole room," Mr. Toppan said approvingly. "Now, bring me my knife and some rags, and mix me a drop or two of yellow wash. I'll tend to the slip while you go on laying the lower wainscot."

It was not easy to correct the line that had wavered, but Mr. Toppan worked quietly until he had done it; then he called Jared to him and explained the method.

"But you'll not slip another line, Jared. There's never any need to, once you see it that way."

Jared smiled up at him. "I know that now, sir."

It was the end of May, and the tide of spring had nearly met that of summer when the room was finished. Cinnamon John could now be brought to it for his first glimpse of the decorated walls, and the party he had planned to celebrate them would soon be in full swing.

Mr. Toppan and Jared stood by the door and their eyes encircled the room with a last loving glance. Mr. Toppan turned to Jared, putting his hand on the boy's shoulder.

"Jared, I've told you a mint of things that you'll probably forget, but the words don't matter if the doing has become part of you. One thing more I'll say–"

"Yes, sir?" Jared looked up expectantly.

"We think the room is fine because we did it, and because we've lived with it all these weeks, and because we've done our best; but it may be that others won't think so."

"Oh, Mr. Toppan, but how could–" Jared began.

Mr. Toppan waved his hand in the air. "Let it be, boy, let it be. Can't you see that it doesn't matter what the world thinks if you've done your work the best you knew how to do?"

Amazement was written wide on the boy's face; then a smile gave it place. "Yes, sir, I do see what you mean."

"I doubt if there's much more I can teach you after this, Jared, but we'll work together on every job as man and man." He turned and pushed the door open. "Now, to find Cinnamon John."

It was the hour before sunset and the light was its warmest and purest when they brought Cinnamon John up to the room. The big man stepped over the threshold with awe in his footsteps. He approached the center of the room as reverently as if it were a shrine, and then he stood still. His breath was short and husky. He brushed one of his big hands across his eyes as if to assure himself that he could not brush away what he was seeing. He turned slowly and took in the whole room; then he turned again and took in every detail of the work.

"Do you think he likes it?" Jared whispered excitedly to Mr. Toppan as they stood in the doorway.

Mr. Toppan inclined his head slightly and laid a finger on his lips. Jared understood that for the moment or these many moments, he would have to remain as still as the brushes in their pot.

Cinnamon John was embraced by yellow walls whose glow stirred an answering glow within him. His eyes were raised first to the frieze near the ceiling–a series of blue waves, rising, curving, falling into fragments of foam. Round the room the frieze went rising, falling, breaking, a repetitive pattern but with such movement and grace that Cinnamon John saw himself as the captain he never became, sailing the uncharted seas of fancy. The same frieze, but in smaller detail, broke around each window in the room and the two doorways.

His eye dropped to the wainscot. Here was a row of pineapples, perfect in form, green with a base of green and a tuft of foliage above them. Wherever the wainscot went, all around the room, the pineapples rested on it. Not too closely spaced, but saying clearly enough to every one that beheld them, "Here is such hospitality as never flowed in any portion of the globe!"

In the panels between the windows were the graceful sweeping boughs of laden fruit trees, blue trees with fruits of red and green, each tree patterned alike. There were spaces where flowers bloomed, but exotic flowers such as no untraveled eye had ever seen.

On the wide panels over the fireplaces at each end of the room, Mr. Toppan had laid one design and no other; and the spacing of it had been decided on only after long hours of deliberation. It was an urn filled with flowers, but only those flowers that bloomed in the East and West alike–a tulip, a lily, a carnation, and a spray of lilac. On either side of the urn was a bird of Paradise; like no bird that had ever taken wing from the earth. The proud head was raised high, the delicate feet were firmly set, the long tail swept in a magnificent curve down to the corner of the panel. With the birds and with the flowers, there was that same imposing of colors that made a prism of a plaster wall.

Cinnamon John's eyes had traversed the room. They came now to rest on the big man and the reedy boy standing in the doorway. Cinnamon John wagged his head, and the broad smile that all his friends knew so well started to wreathe his face. He crossed over to them and took Mr. Toppan's hand in both of his.

"I've sailed many a sea in my time but never a one that brought me to such a land as this," he said, shaking the journeyman painter's hand warmly. "I knew you were a good one, Toppan, when I asked you to do it, but I never knew you'd do so good a job. You've earned your silver dollars and the lifelong commendation of Cinnamon John."

"Thank you, John," Mr. Toppan said. "It's been the best job I've ever done, but that's not to say I won't do a better one, someday."

Great were the preparations the next day for the party that evening–the party that was to show the newly decorated room to the countryside. All day long the odors from the kitchen proclaimed the good things that were being baked and mulled and simmered. The children went to the fields for branches and boughs to deck the lower rooms of the inn. Cinnamon John himself waxed the floor of the upper room, as he would let no one else into it. Mr. Toppan took himself to the woods, striding up the hill shortly after breakfast and not striding down again until near supper time. Jared busied himself cleaning the brushes and stencils and paint pots, packing the kit and storing it in the saddlebags. He brought the horses in from pasture and curried them well. The two mares were so fat from the weeks of green grazing that Jared wondered if their saddle girths would go around them. He swept the saddles free of the dust that had seeped over them while they hung in the barn, then rubbed all the leather with tallow. Everything was in readiness for the morning.

By midafternoon the fiddler arrived and was entertained in the kitchen, and by late afternoon carts and carriages and riders on horseback came up to the door of the inn. There was a feast spread on the table in the long room, and when people assembled for it, the whole inn seemed to be blazing with beauty and good cheer.

Then the longed-for hour came. The guests gathered in the passage, ready to go up the stairs, with the fiddler leading them. Cinnamon John came behind the fiddler, holding by the hand his pretty sixteen-year-old daughter, whose rustling silk dress had come from Persia. Mr. Toppan was next, with the hand of Cinnamon John's wife in his. She was plump and short, he was big and brawny; but merriment made them a pair. So on up the stairs came the crowd, with the fiddler playing rollicking sea tunes, through the open door, and into the room.

Jared, standing by the door with a knot of smaller children, watched it all with the comfort of invisibility given by youth.

Praise mounted from white throats and roared from bearded lips as the stenciled walls were seen; laughter rang and approval boomed. Then the fiddler took his place, tucked his fiddle more closely under his chin, and his music swirled over the crowd like the waves of the frieze.

When the fiddler stopped, voices echoed in the room while the music still hung lightly on the air. "A cheer for Mr. Toppan!" Cinnamon John cried out, raising his husky arm high.

"A cheer for Mr. Toppan!" cried the merrymakers.

Mr. Toppan lifted his hand. "One moment, ladies and gentlemen!"

He broke through the crowd and went toward the doorway where the children clustered. There was such silence in the room that the flickering of candles seemed almost like sound. Mr. Toppan stopped before his apprentice and with a sweep of his great arm drew the boy into the center of the room.

He smiled at the people. "A cheer for Mr. Toppan is not enough," he said; "a cheer for Mr. Toppan and his apprentice it must be!"

A shout led by Cinnamon John went up from the crowd, and Jared, feeling the comfortable weight of Mr. Toppan's strong hand on his shoulder, stood tall. He could forget his ill-fitting suit of coarse homespun cloth, with the bits of paint on it here and there; he could forget, too, the icy wind that had blown across his life and made him shiver even when the sun was high. For here was warmth: joy like a fire that he could hold his hands to and beauty like a bright flame. He smiled into the friendly faces and then looked up at Mr. Toppan.

"We had a good time working on these walls, didn't we, sir?" he said in a whisper.

"That we did, Jared, and they're but the first of many," Mr. Toppan answered. He gave the boy's shoulder a pat and turned him toward the door. "We've an early start to make in the morning; so go you to your bed soon."

Jared nodded and started wending his way through the crowd back to the group of children. They were growing heavy-eyed, and the head of the littlest one drooped with sleep. Jared herded them together like a tired flock, down the stairs, through the kitchen with its lingering aroma of spice, up the steep back stairs to the loft. The children were wordless in their weariness and readily sought their beds under the eaves, crawling into them with boots and clothes that would have stayed on had not Jared helped them to change.

Finally the room was still, save for the breathing of the children. In the distance, almost as if in another world, was the lilt of music and the soft sound of voices that were music in themselves. The night was warm, and Jared lay on the bed without drawing the quilt over him. The moon threw a silver cloak across his shoulders and before it was withdrawn, he was asleep.

There was little stir in the inn the next morning when Cinnamon John gave Mr. Toppan and his apprentice their breakfast. Guests who had remained overnight were still abed, and even Cinnamon John's wife and the children were asleep. While the silver dollars were being counted out, Jared went for the horses, heaving all his strength into securing the saddle girths around their fat bellies. He led them to the doorstep of the inn. The brown mare neighed with eagerness when she saw her master, for she was too used to the road to like the pasture for long. The Gray One, to whom every-thing was still so new, pricked up her ears and pawed the earth with an impatient forefoot.

Cinnamon John put his hand on Jared's shoulder and looked up at Mr. Toppan.

"Toppan," he said, "I've done my best, but I haven't put a mite of flesh on the boy these weeks he's been with us."

"No one can say you haven't tried," Mr. Toppan answered, taking the mare's bridle and swinging his big body lightly into the saddle.

Jared thought of the breads and beans and puddings that had come from the oven, of the great roasts from the spit, and the tasty stews from the iron kettle. "I never knew food could be so good," he said apologetically for his thinness; then he turned and swung his leg over the saddle.

"Good's one thing and useful's another," Cinnamon John muttered. "I'd like to see some flesh on your bones."

"He's not made to get heavy, John," Mr. Toppan said consolingly. "Some folks have heart, and some have body, and some have both. I'm not worrying about a lad with heart. We'll be back one day. Good-bye for now."

The horses were moving ahead, Jared urging the Gray One to keep pace with the mare.

"You'll find no better welcome anywhere," Cinnamon John called after them, his voice deep in his throat; then he turned into his kitchen to stir up the fire for his guests.

They were off and the road reached long before them, winding and mysterious.

"Where are we going now, Mr. Toppan?" Jared asked.

"I don't know, boy. Some place where people want what we can give."

Chapter Four

The road taken by Jared and Mr. Toppan led not only through the country but through the years as they painted their way from one state to another and from one season to the next, leaving their traces across the countryside. Instead of carrying rolls of wallpaper, as some itinerants did, they would stop at a house and unroll their paint kit and bundles of stencils. Some people would want to have one room done, some every room in the house; some would have nothing at all to do with the journeyman painter and his apprentice, but these were lessening with the years.

The gales of war blew across the Atlantic in 1812 as men once again took up their muskets to fight the British. The brief but bloody war soon gave way to peace, and in its wake, progress and prosperity spread across the land. Roads were opened and waterways established. Waterpower was harnessed and factories sprang up. Frontiers expanded until there seemed no limit to what the young nation might achieve.

As the arduous toil of clearing the wilderness and subduing the land diminished, refinements were possible and art became a partner with life. The ornamentation of homes through color and design was now considered as essential as the protection of homes against enemy intrusion had been earlier. The frivolous things of life, which were gracious too, were no longer confined to the cities or to a wealthy few, for peddlers and journeymen of every description were carrying them through the countryside.

Books and trinkets and tinware, gadgets and trifles, even delicacies for the table, as well as all manner of "Yankee notions" were being distributed far and wide. The itinerants might stay anywhere from a few hours to a few days, or even for a few weeks, as in the case of workmen like Mr. Toppan and Jared. The journeyman was a social figure, with words a part of his commerce, and he was always welcome. News of life in the towns, of fashions and society, was relished by women in the country; and men listened eagerly to the tales of those who had journeyed West, tales of rich land without stones, of smooth rivers without boulders. After hearing them, many an adventuresome youth–tired of the struggle with stubborn New England soil–would pack his few belongings in a saddlebag and, taking gun and horse, start West.

Any itinerant workman in those days was prepared to do all kinds of work. Mr. Toppan would often tell a prospective employer that he would be glad to paint anything from the walls of a house inside or out to some trifling decoration; and he often did small jobs, such as clock faces and mirror panels. So much money was his charge, if the work was acceptable, and their board. But there were times when, with winter coming on or a spell of bad weather threatening, they were glad enough to work just for board. Sometimes they would strike a profitable section–western Massachusetts proved to be such–and they would work from one house to the next, well received and well paid, till there wasn't a house in the whole countryside but had its decorated room. There were other times when they went like nomads from one county to the next before anyone wanted their work. Rumors of new houses being built, or of old houses being improved, would send them seeking to ply their trade where many hands were working.

All during the years of itinerating they were never alone, for tides of workmen of all trades traveled with them–

peddlers of every kind of ware, carpenters with their tools, shoemakers with their kits, preachers with their Bibles, doctors on rounds that covered whole counties, judges on their circuits. These were the men who, though none of them knew it, were knitting the country together, linking one town to another and, through trade and commerce, securing the unity of a nation.

Mr. Toppan and Jared, like all the other journeymen, went through the fair days of summer as well as the wind and rain of autumn, the hail and snow and biting cold of winter, and the mud of spring. They went through the green valleys, over passes in the mountains, and, in a land where bridges were few, forded the rivers. It was one thing to lie out at night in the summertime with the stars warm overhead, head pillowed on saddlebags and no covering but the soft air blanketing the earth; it was another to lie out on a stormy night, wet, weary and hungry, falling short of an objective and having to seek shelter along the roadside, holding the horse by the bridle lest the noise of the storm frighten him to flee in the dark.

The day's objective was generally an inn, and there were plenty spread well along the roadways. An inn was a warm and friendly place, alive with good food and good talk, a place where men could swap ideas and even possessions, for it was the spirit of the day to share everything alike. Apples were there in wooden bowls, and popcorn, and plenty to drink during the storytelling.

Often far more than talk echoed around the spacious hearth. Entertainers traversed the countryside too, and put up at the inns–men with puppet shows or fiddles, men with hand organs and carved wooden figures on the top that danced to the music, actors seeking jobs and able to recite long pages of Shakespeare to enraptured audiences, and ventriloquists sitting quietly in corners who could make the chicken in the pot crow as if it were sunrise, or the pig roasting on the spit say all manner of complaining things.

The bristles on Mr. Toppan's brushes wore down and had to be replaced; the packets of dry color were used up and had to be renewed again and again. Jared grew tall and ceased to be a boy looking into the world of men, but a man in his own right. His pale face put on no color except when summer bronzed him, and his body still remained lean; but he was strong and sinewy, and his eyes looked out on his fellows with something new in their dreamy gaze. He was now used to measuring himself up to a job. He knew how warm a thing praise could be, and even in the bitterest days of winter, he who had always felt the cold so, found that appreciation wrapped him like a cloak. He had forgotten, almost forgotten, what fear was; rarely now did that convulsive shivering he had known since he was a child, rack him. The stripling thrill he had felt at being an apprentice had given way to the confident strength of being a master workman.

Five years and more had passed, and during that time he had lost count of the rooms they had done throughout Massachusetts, Connecticut, Rhode Island, and even at one short period, in New York State. In their designs they had used the pineapple motif often, for it was the desire of the day to show hospitality; the willow was another favorite, exquisite and drooping, emblematic of immortality. Sunbursts were often asked for, and bells that rang for joy or liberty.

Sometimes, a simple rose medallion with finely indented leaves laid on a wall divided into panels by a graceful entwining vine was all a room contained, but if the walls were raspberry red, and the designs grass green, they had a way of quickening the whole house. A frieze repeated often was that of the holly encircling a pine and a candle; and always in a house where more than one room was done, a frieze of swags and bells with pendant tassels would be stenciled somewhere. Leaves were familiar motifs, and flowers–tulips that had the nodding grace of springtime, roses with the fullness of summer.

They were New England craftsmen and could use only those designs adaptable to their tools and to the houses of which they would be a part. Though many of the ideas may have originated in other lands, they had now become one with the rolling fields and rocky coasts and tree-clad mountains of their own land. Roses and tulips, blue cornflowers and spicy pinks bloomed in New England gardens, and the lush long branches of willows bent over New England brooks. These were patterns that could be carried into houses and laid upon walls as freely as a woman could pick flowers in her garden and arrange them in a bowl to grace her table.

Once a traveling scholar they met at an inn asked to see Mr. Toppan's stencils. Thumbing through them, he held up the carnation spray and started in a long-winded way to identify it with ancient symbolism.

"You have been influenced by the Orient, I can see," he said. "Tell me now, where did you study and what is your source for these designs?"

Jared, for the first time in his life, saw a look of absolute bewilderment on Mr. Toppan's face.

"Why, they just come natural to me," the journeyman painter said finally, "from where I cannot say."

"Strange, very strange," the scholar murmured.

"Mayhap the beauty that runs through the ages is the same stream," Mr. Toppan went on, gazing into the fire, "just as every flower that unfolds its petals reflects the bloom of creation."

The scholar muttered to himself as he turned the stencils. Mr. Toppan was silent, with a smile upon his face; and Jared thought of the bubbling spring he had seen long ago, coming up out of the earth.

Jared liked best the houses they did for brides, houses being built by husbands-to-be with brawn and love driving every nail. Small red hearts would be delicately or boldly brought into the designs, perhaps hidden in the frieze, or perhaps displayed clearly on the panel over the fireplace. Jared, at work on a pattern of hearts, hummed to himself on his ladder, with his stencil firm and his brush strokes swift. He thought of Jennet then and of what five years would have done for her. Lovely she must be by now, perhaps as tall as her mother, but with her hair still loose on her shoulders and her feet still bare.

Mr. Toppan surveyed the room, the room into which a bride would soon be brought. There was color and life in it, and something more to deck that first night under the roof where all nights thereafter would be spent.

"It's a pretty greeting for a wedded lass, isn't it, Mr. Toppan?" Jared commented. He smiled to himself, thinking of the day when he would do a room just so and then lead Jennet into it–her room, his wife, forever and a day.

"Boy, it's not a greeting; it's a symbol of all that these four walls shall embrace."

Mr. Toppan turned to Jared, but someone new was standing in the room, someone unfamiliar save for the brushes in his hand. Jared's head was high, a smile lived in his face. It was as if the beauty he had brought to drab gray walls for five years past had given strength and vitality to his thin bones and pale skin.

"I can't call you boy anymore, Jared," Mr. Toppan said slowly. "You've grown a man."

Jared was cleaning his stencil and Mr. Toppan was bending over the kit, packing it for their journey.

"Marriage must be a fine thing, Mr. Toppan. Why did you never take a wife?"

"I did, Jared, and for nearly a year we had a home and some land. I was a farmer with no thought then of a stencil kit; but death was quicker than life." He stopped. His voice was quiet, neither heavy nor sad. He was relating a fact, not probing a wound.

"My father found another wife after my mother died," Jared said.

Mr. Toppan nodded. "Some men can, Jared, and the world must bless them for being sensible; but some men love once and never love again, for they still love that one. You're that kind, Jared. You'll love but once and, when you do, God grant that she love you."

Jared stood motionless in the room that was filling up with twilight, the little red hearts still showing bright on the walls. A cold wind swept around him and he shivered. Putting down his brushes, he took his coat from a peg and pulled it on; but he had learned long ago that no coat could warm him when that wind blew.

There was one more job to do before the winter set in for certain. As they rode through the golden richness of October, Mr. Toppan told Jared of it.

"We've a free hand here, Jared. The order is for a decorated room with plenty of design and color. Squire Tallant is away and, but for a servant or two, we'll have the place to ourselves; so–" he raised his arm and threw a sweeping gesture around the autumn world, "here is our pattern. Shall we do it? And, what's more, let's satisfy the Squire's feeling for heraldry."

Squire Tallant was one of the old Tories who had learned to guard their words after the Revolution, but he still kept his coat of arms over the fireplace in the great room of his house. It was the parlor he wanted decorated, a good-sized, six-windowed room. And, as Mr. Toppan explained, the Squire did not care what the design was so long as it was something he could understand. His memory reached back to the brightly wallpapered rooms in England, and his desire was to see a room in his own house reminiscent of them.

That night, after supper had been served to the journeyman and his apprentice, Mr. Toppan told Jared the story of heraldic symbolism: how a coat of arms might be won by a noble family for being valiant or in the royal favor, and how their descendants had the right to use it perpetually. Jared listened in fascination. Mr. Toppan's mind was like a storehouse full of unexpected knowledge, for he seemed to have some learning about everything. Jared had commented on it more than once, and Mr. Toppan had laughed.

"When you have sat around as many hearths as I have," he said in explanation, "you'll have as much information. But it's only oddments."

Mr. Toppan, however, was not to work on those walls. The next day, when they were spacing the frieze with cord and chalk, the ladder he was standing on slipped, and he fell heavily to the floor. Jared hurried to help him to his feet but, unlike other falls that happened occasionally, he could not be assisted.

"It's my back, Jared, feeling as if it were being twisted the wrong way around."

Jared sought one of the servants and between them they carried Mr. Toppan to his bed, a bed they thought he would leave in a few hours, but which he did not leave for a month. During the days while Jared waited for Mr. Toppan to resume the work, he made some preliminary preparations, but after a week Mr. Toppan urged his apprentice to do the work himself.

" 'Twill take longer than if we were both at it, but you know enough to go ahead until I can join you."

"Mr. Toppan, we haven't made any designs yet. I–"

"Jared," the big man said with difficulty, "you can stand still in that room until those four walls talk to you. Think of what means most to Squire Tallant. Do that, and speak the things you have learned through the work. Now leave me, lad. I'm not at ease, and like the dumb creatures, I can bear a touch of suffering better if I bear it alone."

Jared's heart felt heavy when he left the room. All the years he had worked as Mr. Toppan's apprentice he had relied on him. Now he was brought up sharp with the realization that he must bear the work himself, carry out its conception and its doing just as he would when on his own. Jared went back slowly to the great, bare, six-windowed room with its high fireplace and finely carved mantel. It was late in the afternoon and the autumn light was pale around him, too late to begin work but not too early to begin planning.

He stood quietly, as Mr. Toppan had told him to do, trying to find somewhere that idea which would serve Squire Tallant best. The Squire was as good a patriot as any man, but he still revered his family's coat of arms, clinging to that memorial of other days when glory came of royal patronage and not of a man's two hands hewing out his life from the wilderness.

"Look to nature for your patterns," Mr. Toppan had said many times.

Jared left the house and went across the meadow and up a lane that led into the woods. The low-lying sun had tipped the world and every growing thing with gold. Heraldic streamers of red and gold, sable and green, waved in splendor from oak, maple, beech, and darkling pine.

He breathed deeply and lifted his head high to meet the keen rush of air. Down the golden archway of the year the wind came charging, under the tattered banners of the trees that hung out against the sky like knightly standards flying from gray cathedral walls. This was the glory hour of the trees when, before their leaves fell, they celebrated the passage of the year.

Jared saw with sudden realization that the branches reaching crosswise from stalwart trunks revealed the structure of each tree as a cross. The standards of the knights of old had proclaimed the cross; but those were emblems of a single journey to a distant land, while the cross on which each tree was built was a symbol of a faith that knew no quailing no matter how long its crusading.

The wind struck swiftly, swinging the bright banners to and fro, clutching at bits and sending tatters of the maple's gold, the oak's crimson, the beech's copper into the air, reaching vainly for the pine's dark strength.

The trees quivered and were silent as the wind raged around them; they stood with dark trunks rooted in the earth and crossed boughs held uplifted to the heavens.

As Jared gazed at the boughs, now almost bare, he saw on every twig tight buds outlined against the sunset gold: the crimson secret of the oak, the enscaled cradle of the maple, the little sheathed sword of the beech.

"Faith, my friend," the pine seemed to whisper, "faith has the last word always."

The wind swept low, swirling the leaves in a golden shower, then was gone. Jared stood still with the evening coolness coming out of the woods and washing about him. There was no sound anywhere. He brushed his hand before his eyes. An idea, like a cobweb, had tangled itself in his thoughts, but there were fine strands to it which, if he would follow, could lead him rightly.

He walked back to the house across the dark fields, guided by the amber glow of candlelight shining from one window. Cobweb strands were flimsy things, he thought; he needed far more than cobwebs to secure his idea. He worked late that night cutting his stencils–a whetstone beside him so that his knife might never lose its sharpness; through the days that followed he worked long and earnestly.

Mr. Toppan knew better than to ask him any questions; needless they would have been when Jared's eyes shone with all that he was seeing.

It was harder work than he had ever done, for he was doing it alone; and firm as his fingers were in the mornings, in the late afternoons he often had to stop long before the light waned, because of the numbness in them. He would not risk a single wavering line in this room of his.

He remembered seeing a decorated room at one of the inns–a room in which he could tell by the steadiness of the pattern which work had been done in the morning and which in the latter part of the day. Jared was resolved that no such signature should proclaim his work.

When he had done all he could for the day, he would clean his brushes and stencils, shut the door of the room, and go to the woods.

There, he was rarely alone. Overhead, the indrawn whistle of the harmless broad-tailed hawk could be heard as it floated idly across the sky. Or a flutter of wings and a cheerful prattle would bring a chickadee to hand, alighting on a nearby bush. A squirrel scolded in the branches above, that quick flow of energetic sound that was no more than a torrent of small talk to ease a flighty conscience. The underbrush stirred and a deer darted across the path, but with the swiftness of custom, not of fear. Jared brought to the woods only a longing to learn of the hidden secrets of beauty, and the creatures knew it. A man who used a brush was not one to wield a gun.

"I've seen squirrels seeking nuts all my life," Jared said one evening as he sat with Mr. Toppan, "but never have I seen them in such haste to store them."

"They know best and that's the first sign of many to prepare for a hard winter."

"The brown mare has a coat on her like that of a bear," Jared said with a laugh, "and as for the Gray–I think just being astride her will keep me warm!"

Mr. Toppan smiled. "That's good. You'll find plenty of cold in the north."

"Are we going north this winter?"

"You are, Jared. Your time is more than over with me and you'd do better to start itinerating in the winter than in the spring, I have a way of thinking."

Jared stared into the fire. It was reasonable to find a place where he would have board and lodging for his work during the winter; but it was hard to face the parting, even though he had always known it was to be.

"I'd like to work with you for a while longer, Mr. Toppan," he said.

"I'd like to have you, but it isn't fair. I can't teach you any more and it's time for me to take on another apprentice. Next summer you'll be taking one on."

"I!" Jared exclaimed, amazed at such a thought.

"Why, of course, Jared. Else how should our trade grow unless we teach others?"

Jared was silent for a long time, then he said slowly, "Where should I start to find work?"

"Back north," Mr. Toppan replied with no hesitation. "New Hampshire has had little enough of the stencilers, compared to Massachusetts and Connecticut. You'll find an open field there and one where you'll make your own name with pride. You've been 'Toppan's boy' long enough. It's time for you to be yourself: Jared Austin, the Journeyman Stenciler."

During the next few days, Jared finished his work with mingled feelings–real sorrow that his apprenticeship with Mr. Toppan was over and that any future meeting they might have would be by happenstance; excitement that he was about to try himself, command his own ideas, set his own prices. Aside from the work there was the knowledge that in going back to his own land he would see–perhaps not until next summer, but soon all the same–Jennet and Mother Thaxter, Nancy Austin and the girls, and the baby who must be a fair-sized boy by now.

Because he was a free man in his own right and could no longer be cowed by fear, Jared knew that he could face his father; he even dared to picture his father forgetting all the anguish he had brought to the world. Eben Austin then would look upon his son with respect instead of hatred. Jared would go north when Mr. Toppan said, but he would not go over the mountains into his homeland until spring or summer, not until he had decorated many rooms and could be called a master in his own right, an apprentice no longer.

The day approached when his work on Squire Tallant's walls was done and he could bring Mr. Toppan into the room to see it for himself, for Mr. Toppan had left his bed now and was hearty enough.

Mr. Toppan said nothing when he saw Jared's walls, just as years ago, Cinnamon John had said nothing. He stood still and let the walls embrace him, telling their story. There, on walls washed a grayish hue, were the leaves found in the woods–painted bronze, ocher, and venetian red. They made a frieze so buoyant and alive that the wind seemed to be skipping through them. There was a pine tree balanced truly, dark green and strong, a motif repeated throughout the room. There was a leafless branch encradling buds. The design was simple and serene, and gaiety bordered the whole in the dancing frieze of leaves.

Mr. Toppan turned to Jared. His eyes were glazed with tears. "You have sealed your apprenticeship with great promise," was all he said, but Jared knew what it meant.

There were a few brief happy days before Jared went north. Squire Tallant returned and was so pleased with the room that he not only paid Mr. Toppan well in silver dollars but gave him three more rooms to do which would keep him busy all through the winter. Now Jared was impatient to start on his own and every day kept from it seemed wasted. Mr. Toppan paid him what he had agreed upon, and Squire Tallant added a gift of five silver dollars which would help Jared buy his stenciling kit–paints, brushes, knife, dry powders, and stiff paper.

Squire Tallant had a parting gift for Jared, a bag of corn, which he pressed into the lad's reluctant hands.

" 'Tis the finest Indian corn ever raised," he said, "and worth its weight in gold to a farmer."

"But, sir, I'm no farmer," Jared protested.

"You've got to be something of a farmer to survive," Squire Tallant went on. "Take it, boy; you may find a use for it all the same."

Jared took the bag as if it were a curiosity.

Squire Tallant smiled. "Agriculture lives on seed rather than harvests, and you've got enough in that bag to feed a county, if you use it well."

The early November morning was sunny and warm when Jared threw his saddle over the Gray One's back and stowed the bag of seed away in his saddlebag. A long hand-shake with Mr. Toppan ended five-and-a-half years of apprenticeship.

"Good-bye," he said, then pointed the Gray One's head toward the north and waved his hat in final farewell.

Mr. Toppan, with Squire Tallant standing beside him, watched Jared go. What lay ahead of the lad no man could guess, but Mr. Toppan felt that he had equipped him with a trade that linked heart and hand, and with such he could find his own place in the world.

"God be with you," he called out.

Jared pressed the Gray One forward. The road was long before them and, though the sun was warm, there were heavy clouds edging the sky. The wind snapped a cold lash out of the north.

"We've a hard winter before us," Squire Tallant was saying as the two men turned and went toward the house.

Chapter Five

Jared took three days for his journey into New Hampshire, three days over the winding roads with autumn's dry leaves racing before him and the trees waving dark branches against the sky. The clean fields, lying fallow for next spring's planting, offered him the satisfaction of familiarity; but when the road began to climb and the fields gave place to woodlands and the bare trees to the deep green of the pines, he felt the thrill of remembering things. The air was sharper now, and woven through it was the fragrance of spruce and hemlock.

The first night he spent outdoors comfortably enough, tethering the Gray One and bedding himself down with his saddle for a pillow and his extra coat for a blanket. The second night was far too brisk; so by late afternoon he rode up to a farmhouse on the outskirts of a village and asked shelter for himself and his mare. It was gladly given, and more than one night he might have had for the asking. Jared had no intention of seeking work in that district; so he busied his hands in the evening with painting a design on the glass of the clock face–much to the delight of the farmer's wife and a brood of children. Soon after dawn he was off on the road again. Before him, distant and blue and bordering the northern rim of the world, were the hills which meant home. As the day passed and they came more and more within his range, he could discern the outlines of mountains he knew.

The country had changed since he had last seen it. The clearings were larger and closer together. The villages had grown, and where there had been only a few houses, now there were several; schools had been built, stores, inns, meeting houses. Sheep were grazing over the hillsides where a few years ago only deer and rabbit had run; sleek cattle were standing in the barnyards, luxuriating in the sun as if they knew that soon they would be shut in dark barns away from it. For snow was on the wind; the damp smell of it moistened the air, and winter hung brooding over the land.

Jared reined in the Gray One at a crossroads on a high, bald hilltop. Before him, yet near now and sweetly familiar, were the hills that had been the ramparts of his childhood. The road that led through the pass and into the valley beyond was there for him to take, the road that linked him with all that was dear–his home and that of the Thaxters, Jennet with all her childhood gaiety come to maidenly grace.

"Jennet Thaxter." Jared said the name lovingly, quietly, to the wind. Then, emboldened by memory and his aloneness on the hilltop, he cried out, "Will you marry me, Jennet Thaxter?"

The Gray One flicked her ears and turned her head at the well-known voice that often addressed her during their journeying. The wind sent a handful of leaves over the road and tossed them high. There was no other sound. There never would be an answer to Jared's question until he crossed the mountains and sought it himself from Jennet's lips. But he was not going to cross the mountains; not yet–not until spring had come. He must do work of his own first. He must become Jared Austin, Journeyman Stenciler, and have somewhat to offer Jennet.

So he turned the Gray One's head eastward and away from the mountains, away from the road that might have led back to remembered pastures, and took the other road into the valley. Soon he reached a small village and drew up at the inn. It was not hunger but the need for information that impelled him to the long table in the kitchen. Listening to the talk, he could add some of his own from time to time and find out what he wanted to know.

"Are there many new houses a-building here-abouts?" he asked Dan True, the host, when the time seemed ripe for such a question.

"They have been, lad, like mushrooms, for New Hampshire has been settling fast these few years gone by. But you sound like a New Hampshire man yourself. Where have you been these years?"

Jared told Dan True of his journeying with Mr. Toppan and where it had led them and what they had done.

"I've heard of Mr. Toppan; he's a great one!" True exclaimed. "When is he coming this way? There's many that would welcome his brush in these parts."

"He's sent me this way to see what work there is."

"You!" Dan True looked surprised. "Lad, you don't look strong enough to hold a paint pot."

Jared felt his cheeks tingling. "I'm strong enough, just reedy, and that'll not interfere with my work. Haven't you a room you'd like done? I'll soon show you the best that Mr. Toppan has taught me."

"Maybe I have a room, but I've not got the mind to see it done just yet," True replied cautiously. "Now, why not take yourself a few miles farther on where there's a fine square house John Dunklee built two years past. Beyond that, I'm told, a strapping young farmer is getting a house all readied for his bride."

Jared's eyes danced. "It's a fine thing to do a house for a bride."

Dan True smiled genially. "See what you can do that way this winter. I'll have my room ready for a bit of decoration in the spring."

Jared reached into his pocket for one of the silver dollars Squire Tallant had given him.

Dan True looked at him and shook his head. "Put it back, lad; I wouldn't take your money. That dish of stew you had was hardly worth the news you brought. Come back in the spring. We'll take money then and other things too. Now, go east along this road, less than an hour's journeying, and you'll come to the houses I spoke of, and perhaps a few others. They're prosperous up that way, with the best apple trees around here; and John Dunklee's sheep grow the longest wool in all New Hampshire."

"Which house is his?" Jared asked.

"The first you'll come to, and up the hill from it is the new one now building."

Jared took his leave and was soon trotting over the road with a lightness in his heart. The wind was keen and winter was near, but here was a chance for work to tide him through the winter; and here was a whole countryside of farming folk bringing riches from the land after years of hard labor.

The early dusk of November was seeping over the land when a bend in the road brought before him a well-set two-story house. John Dunklee, its builder, must have understood the art of symmetry, so finely balanced were its windows with the great center doorway and thick central chimney. One room was already warm with candlelight, and the glow of it came out to the night like a friendly hand. Jared reined up at the door. The Gray One, used to waiting, dropped her head to the grass. Standing on the broad granite step, Jared knocked on the heavy wood. There was a stir in the house, the padding of feet in soft shoes crossing a room, then the door was opened.

"Have you shelter for a journeyman this night?" Jared began.

The woman smiled, and with her smile the warmth and the light and the fragrance of a lived-in home came out to greet him.

"Bless you, lad, come in! Is your horse all right? I'll send one of the boys to the barn with it."

Jared stepped into the long room by whose great fireplace pots were simmering and a kettle steaming. Looking out another door, the woman called to a small boy to take the stranger's horse to the barn and bed him down well. Suddenly it seemed like a dream to Jared, for just a few years ago he had been the small boy summoned to take the stranger's horse to the barn.

"John's out milking but he'll be in soon. Sit down and warm yourself and tell me where you're bound."

"I'm not bound anywhere, ma'am; I'm looking for work."

"What kind of work?" Eliza Dunklee asked. There were all sorts of workmen itinerating these days; some of them a farmer could use and some of them he could not, but all of them were worth listening to.

Jared told her he was a stenciler by trade and was looking for unpainted walls that needed a bit of brightening.

Eliza's delight was written large over her face. For two years she had worked hard to bring what beauty she could to the bare walls of the Dunklee farmhouse. The dye-pot had done its best with coloring for her linens and woolens; the flower garden had helped, too, in the growing season; but there were long, dark days in winter when the house seemed drab enough to vex her spirit.

"Tell me, will it cost a mint of money to do our parlor as you say?"

Jared smiled and shook his head. "Can you board me through the winter while I do your walls and perhaps the walls of other houses hereabouts?"

She nodded. "Is that all you ask? Then you shall have the best that we can give you."

As they talked, three children came in and sat cross-legged by the fire, listening with eager ears to all that was being said and eyeing longingly the pack at Jared's feet in which his tools were stowed. John Dunklee entered. Placing his milk pail down carefully, he strode across the room with right hand outstretched.

"Welcome, friend," was his greeting to Jared.

Eliza spoke fast, the children chiming in with her, all of them eager to tell Jared's story for him.

"I've heard about this from Massachusetts men," Dunklee said slowly, "and I've vowed to myself that 'twas time New Hampshire started to dress houses up a bit."

Jared smiled. What a change had taken place since Mr. Toppan had tried to persuade Eben Austin to have his walls done! But then, life had prospered, and toil was going hand in hand with enjoyment, and people could afford beauty.

"I'm proud to have you begin with our house, Jared Austin," Dunklee went on, "–the parlor first, and then yonder small bedroom where the children are born."

Eliza smiled proudly at his mention of the parlor, the room that spoke of her best, that held her Chelsea china and Staffordshire ware–those fragile things her grandmother had brought from England and which, because they were so loved, had lived through two generations of pioneering life. Her smile deepened with wistfulness as she thought of the small room where three high voices had already made their first demands and where another voice would be heard, come spring–the room of anguish and bliss so linked that they were one.

"John," Eliza said, turning quickly to her husband, "could he work first on the borning room?"

"But Eliza, the parlor–" John began, then he knew what she meant. Those who came to the parlor had come often and would come often again. The one who came to the borning room must have a first sight that would be forever memorable.

They had their supper at the long table by the hearth–noggins of fresh milk and maize bread with blueberries in it, potatoes roasted in the ashes, apples in an earthen dish, and nuts that the children nibbled on like squirrels.

"I've not yet seen such a heavy weight of nuts as the trees have borne this year," John Dunklee commented.

"They were saying the same thing farther south," Jared said. " 'Tis nature's providing against a hard winter."

"Well, I've my barn full of hay and enough wood cut and dried for a year. Your mare won't starve or your fingers freeze while you're working on the Dunklee house."

"I've got no fear of starving or of freezing either," Jared said quietly.

Dishes were removed and the table cleared for Jared to spread out his stencils and discuss his plans for the walls.

Everyone had ideas, from the Dunklee parents, through Reuben and Delight, to Tobit, the youngest boy. Finally they decided on a wash of warm yellow ocher for the walls of the parlor, since it was a north room and cried for warmth. Jared was to be allowed to lay on what stencil he chose. The borning room was to have its walls washed over with gray, then a clambering vine would divide the walls into panels, and in each panel–under the frieze with bells and above the wainscot with its delicate border of intertwining leaves–was to be placed one single rose with its petals wide open. That was Jared's idea and Eliza had listened enraptured as he drew the picture of it in words.

"Why just one rose?" Dunklee asked. "I'd like to see several in each panel."

Jared shook his head; then he picked up his stencil kit and one of the uncut sheets of stiff paper. Working slowly and carefully, as if five people were not watching him, he traced his design and cut out his stencil of a rose. Then he mixed a small amount of paint and on a flat board brought the rose to life. He moved away from the table and held it against the wall.

"Can you see it this way now?" he asked.

The rose was bright and pleasing; its open petals seemed to give out fragrance. Eliza recalled the roses she had coaxed into bloom in her garden. John remembered the wild roses growing by the brook, singly and stately. Rare things made one think deeply because they were not too easily obtained.

Tobit, leaning against his mother, was getting sleepy. Seeing the rose, he opened his eyes wide and said, "It's a real rose, Mama, isn't it? I want to smell it."

Dunklee smiled. "Have it your own way, Jared. Place what you will, where you will."

Jared was given a corner in the big room where he could mix his jars of paint, and a room upstairs where he could sleep. The next day he began his work on the Dunklee walls. The house was quiet during the day but not silent, for soft sounds of industry throbbed through it as Eliza fulfilled her household tasks.

Some days the whizz of the shuttle and the clatter of treadles echoed through the rooms as she worked at the loom. Other days Jared moved his brush to the buzz of the wheel and the creak of the windle as wool was spun and wound. One day a week there was always the thumping of butter being churned. Then there were tasks whose accompaniment was not sound but fragrance–the nourishing smell of baking and the oily smell as candles were molding.

Sometimes, on a stormy afternoon when the children had worked long enough and there was no chance for them to go outdoors and play, Eliza gathered them around her on the hearth, and her voice could be heard as she read to them from the Bible.

Every night John Dunklee appraised Jared's work as it took shape and the drab walls began to come alive. In a few weeks the borning room had been transformed into a bower, and its narrow walls no longer seemed to converge around the small bed but to open out onto vistas of beauty. The children loved to stand quietly in that room, for the pictures on the walls were stories that seemed capable of constant retelling.

By mid-December, winter came on hard and relentless. Snow blew thick and fast in a series of blizzards, and there were many days when the only traffic around the house was to the barn and back. Huge logs blazed all day on the hearth, and at night the coals were banked carefully with ashes, ready to be fanned into flame in the morning.

Jared had heard often of the young farmer up the road who was building a house for his bride, and when the Dunklee walls were done he had thought to go there and seek to decorate some of the house. But news of the Dunklee walls was echoing around the countryside, and Jared knew he would have small need to seek work in that community, for it was seeking him. One winter afternoon when the fading light made work no longer possible, Jared was sitting by the hearth carving a wooden horse for Tobit. The crunch of feet on the hard-packed snow could be heard outside; then the door was flung open. A blast of bitter air preceded the entrance of Corban Cristy. Even in the large room he towered, and his voice boomed loudly enough to shake the pewter on the dresser.

"So, you're the stenciler." He held out his hand to Jared. "I'm Cristy, up the road a mile. It's cold and getting colder." He drew a chair up to the fire and loosened his coat.

"Yes, I'm a stenciler," Jared said. "I do walls for those who have an eye for such."

Cristy pushed back his chair and started roaming around the room. He stood in the doorway of the small bedroom leading off the kitchen, surveying the gray walls with their grass-green leaves and cherry-bright flowers. He was a powerfully built man, with broad shoulders that nearly touched the doorposts, and a proud head with a mane of heavy black hair. His arms hung supple and strong at his sides, the arms of a man who had grappled with the wilderness and subdued it. His stance, well anchored but ready always to move forward, was that of a man who had made his own terms with life, getting what he demanded and giving what he cared.

Tobit had run over beside him. "They're real roses, Mr. Cristy; don't you want to smell them?"

Cristy nodded. "It's good work, and it will please a woman's fancy. Now, let's see your other room."

"It's not finished–" Jared began, loath as Mr. Toppan had always been to have anything seen before it was complete.

"What's that to me?" Cristy boomed out. "Let's see the room."

Jared opened the door that led into the parlor. Two walls were done; a third was in process of doing. Jared felt embarrassed. It was as if the room were not properly clothed and he wished to apologize for it. The Dunklees had seen the walls at all stages, but with them it had been different, for they knew what the finished room would be like.

Cristy nodded his head. "What's your price, Austin?"

"I'd have to see your rooms first," Jared answered. He felt small beside this strapping farmer, and the cold of the day was seeping into the house. He shivered.

"Come along with me and I'll show you; we can talk business later."

Jared nodded. The day was growing old and the cold was deepening as it did toward evening, but here was a man who would brook no delay. Jared smiled as he put his coat on and pulled his cap down over his ears. Mr. Toppan would have been the first to say that when seeking work one had to forget oneself and remember only the man with work to give.

They trudged out into the cold together, along the winding road where ox teams, lugging wood to the village, had made a track. Corban Cristy was full of talk–of the house he had finished and of the bride from a nearby settlement that he would bring there in early summer. His voice softened when he spoke of "the lass," and during the months Jared worked for him he was never to hear her referred to by any other name than "the lass." As Jared came to know Cristy better he heard "the mare" and "the ewe" referred to in almost the same way. There was work for male and female in Cristy's world; one was for strength, the other for generation. But mention of "the lass" or "the ewe" or "the mare" never failed to call forth a kind of gentleness from the big man with his deep voice and ranging stride.

Now the house stood before them, on a rise of land above the road, and set so that it looked across Cristy's open fields to the rim of woods and the dip to the valley. It was a small house, a true New Hampshire farmhouse with wide front door and double windows spaced on either side, squat center chimney and roof of split pine shakes. Cristy's prosperity was proclaimed to the community, for he had painted his house white. Most farmers let the wood of their houses weather to gray, or they used red–the cheapest and hardest-wearing paint. But Corban Cristy's house was white. A fine barn stood near the house, and from it came a faint chorus of cattle lowing and sheep baaing.

Cristy opened the wide front door, and Jared followed, stepping into the small entryway. On one side was a square, three-windowed room with a low-manteled fireplace; on the other side was the kitchen, taking up half the house with its great hearth. At the back of the house was a buttery with shelves lining the walls and a small bedroom. The house, built around the center chimney, was simple and functional in its design. A flight of steep stairs–sixteen treads since she was a bride who would first come to the house–led up to a loft where yet another room could be finished.

Jared stood in the loft and heard the structure of the house tell its own story, from the massive ridgepole raised with the help of Cristy's neighbors to the hewn timbers and stalwart crossbeams that had been felled by Cristy's ax in the woods and dragged here by his oxen. The chimney, rising through the roof, had been made of bricks shaped by knowing hands and baked in a kiln near the village. Here was the story of a man working with the strength of his hands and the aid of nature and the love of a woman. Jared sighed. God grant that his hands might add their skill to it.

"When the children come I'll make a fine room up here," Cristy was saying.

They went back down the steep stairs. The house was cold and filling up quickly with darkness. Cristy lit a lantern and took Jared from room to room.

Cristy laughed deeply as they stood in the kitchen. "Smoke will decorate the walls soon enough in this room, but yonder entry–you can do something pretty there, and the square front room–that's a woman's pride and 'twill be the lass's. I want a house as fine for her as the land is for me, and there's no land finer in all the state; I work it all myself."

"I'll do walls you'll like," Jared said with conviction, "for to do a bride's house has been my longing for a good while now."

Cristy laughed again. " 'Twouldn't be all men's, but I'm glad it's yours."

Jared smiled. "I like to think of the time I'll bring my bride to a house I've made beautiful for her."

The wind was whistling outside and the fireless house was cold, but they stood for a while longer in the kitchen, making their bargain. When the Dunklee work was done, Jared was to begin on Corban Cristy's walls but continue living at the Dunklees'. Two rooms Jared was to do, each one to be paid in dollars, since no lodging was to be given until spring; and as there was no need for the house to be ready until June, Jared could work on other jobs in the neighborhood if they came to him. One thing Corban Cristy made Jared swear to–that no stencil used in his house would have been used before or would ever be used again.

"I want the lass to have something the like of no one else's," Cristy said.

So Jared promised to cut new stencils for the Cristy house and to destroy them when his work was done.

They clasped hands on the bargain and went out the door, Cristy swinging his lantern toward the barn to tend his stock for the night, Jared turning down the white road to follow the narrow track made by the ox teams. The sharp wind cut through his clothes and penetrated his thin body; but he was happy, and happiness had a warmth of its own for him.

The year was almost as old as it was ever allowed to be, and the new year of 1816 was close at hand. Jared, looking down it, saw work opening out for him. He saw his reputation growing, reaching out, perhaps reaching over the mountains to the west so that the people in those villages would be sending for him to come do their houses. Then Jennet would hear of his coming long before he came, and she would remember that when they were younger he had said he would come back for her.

Eliza had kept some hasty pudding for Jared since it was long past the supper hour. "Bless you, Jared," she cried in relief when he entered. "I thought you were never coming– and such a night as it is!"

"It's never been so cold, not as long as anyone around here can remember," John Dunklee said slowly, "but Cristy is like that. He gets an idea and has to push it through; can't even wait for the light of day to talk painted walls, I'll wager."

Jared moved near the fire. He opened his lips, but they were stiff with the cold and would hardly shape the words he wanted to say. After he had warmed a bit he told the Dunklees of the work before him.

John nodded. "I'm glad, Jared. Corban Cristy is a good farmer and has done well. He'll pay you all you deserve, perhaps more, but watch that you don't draw his ire. He's flighty, and he's got a temper beside which an explosion of granite is like the splitting of a seed pod."

"That won't be new to me." Jared smiled stiffly, thinking of Eben Austin and his dark rages.

John Dunklee feared to leave the fire on such a night; so Jared, eager to start outlining stencils, agreed to sit by it and keep it ablaze.

"If it gets much colder we'll all be sleeping in this one room," Dunklee said as he went to bed.

Midnight came and went. The cold crept around the edges of the kitchen so that Jared found his hand unsteady with shivering. He climbed upstairs and one by one brought the children down, wrapped in their blankets, and laid them near the hearth. They stirred a little and Tobit whimpered, but

Jared knew the warmth would give them better dreams. He went out to the barn. It had a damp warmth as the animals threw off steam from their heavy-coated bodies. The chickens were roosting on the backs of the cattle to keep their feet from freezing. Jared hurried to the house through the night that felt so brittle it seemed that a breath would break it; but the breath caught in his throat. He heaped logs on the fire and sat on the hearth near the blaze, in one hand, a piece of paper, and in the other, a piece of charcoal for sketching.

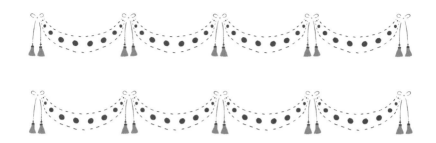

Chapter Six

That night, instead of being the first of a cold spell, was the first of a long succession of such nights. When the weather showed no sign of moderating, a way of life was made to adapt to it. Before the week was out, the Dunklee family were all sleeping in the long room, and Jared and John were taking watches between them through the night to keep the fire and have an eye on the barn. The animals were moved into even closer quarters so that the heat they threw off might be more confined.

Jared worked during the daytime to finish the parlor walls of the Dunklee house, for with his sketches for the Cristy house nearing completion, he was eager to start on it. There was little warmth in the square room but Jared seemed to feel the cold less than most people; only when his brushes stiffened and his paints hardened so that they would not flow would he seek the fire in the kitchen. It had burned so long that the bricks were warm as sun-baked granite in a summer field, and Jared, laying his hands on them, felt heat flow into fingers that had become almost as stiff as his bristles.

"It's the longest cold spell I've ever seen," John Dunklee said as January drew to its close and there had been no letup in the weather.

Only on days when snow came blowing on the wind, piling up more inches on the five feet that already blanketed the country, did the cold mitigate a little; then the next day it would come on again, steelier than ever, with muffled quietness except for the creaking of the trees and the whispering sound of hard snow contracting. In the house there would be the snap of a board splitting or a nail cracking; then silence again. There was another sound and it was one that cut to the heart–the pitiful lowing from the barn of creatures that could not be warm. So they took to bringing the cows and sheep into the house for brief periods.

"Down the village way this past month, there's more than one farmer has lost his newborn calves from the cold," Dunklee said. "My brown cow is ready to calve, and I can't afford to lose her–or the young one either." Worry plowed a furrow across his brow.

"I've helped many a calf into the world on my father's farm," Jared said. "We'll bring the brown cow through."

"It must have been the Lord who sent you here this winter," Dunklee exclaimed, "for what I'd be doing alone in all this cold I don't know–what with the children so small and Eliza not fit right now for much hard work."

Jared smiled. No flames on a hearth ever sent such a rush of warmth through his body as did words of appreciation.

"You've not got overmuch flesh on you," Dunklee went on, "but you don't seem to feel the cold like most folks. 'Tis beyond me the way you work in that parlor till your paints are ice, the way you milk in the barn when the milk has all but frozen in your pail. And when you sleep or what you eat, I don't know. But I'm glad to have you here." He took up his pail that had been warming by the fire and went out to the milking.

Jared went on with his work, singing quietly to himself for pleasure at the room that had come into its perfect bloom. Only small finishing touches remained to be done here and there. It was a warm room, with spruce yellow walls that kept their cheer even against the stark white country that peered in at each of the four windows. His colors were the red of bricks and the green of marsh rushes. The willow design that he had made was graceful; interspersed were small, intricately developed medallions that followed no set pattern. Yes, it was beautiful, the best yet that he had done. He smiled to himself as he heard Mr. Toppan saying, "That's not to say I can't do a better." And that better for Jared would be the house Corban Cristy was making for his bride.

The door opened and shut quickly, and feet moved hastily across the long room and toward the parlor.

"Jared!" Eliza Dunklee was standing in the doorway.

He turned quickly. Her large cape was wrapped tightly around her, but under it she was shivering. Her face was pale, as if all color had been driven from it by the icy wind, and her eyes were wild and frightened. Jared had seen the eyes of a deer look like that when driven by hunters out of the woods.

"Eliza, what is it?" Jared crossed quickly toward her and, taking her hands, led her to the fire and made her sit down on the settle.

" 'Tis cold enough to freeze the marrow in your bones," she said, her teeth chattering against the words.

Jared rubbed her hands in his, for the cold had drained the heat from her body like a fluid, and there was little vitality left to catch the warmth from the fire. But it was not the cold alone that had made her numb and chilled. It was something far worse. It was fear. Jared saw in her eyes the look of one who had fled fear but had been overtaken by its stealthy stalking.

"Oh, Jared–" The words came with a rush, then were choked, then came hastily again. "I've been down in the valley at the Prestons'. Nancy had her babe this morning–but she couldn't give it life–they said she was so cold–oh, Jared, no matter how much wood the men put on the fire, they couldn't get the room warm. . . . " The shaking of Eliza's body and the clicking of her teeth drowned the rest of her words.

Jared kept rubbing her hands together between his own until the shivering lessened. Eliza's head, which she had held tensely against the settle, bent forward; her eyes, which had been glazed with fright, swam in a mist of sadness.

"Poor mite of a babe," she said in a softer tone. "I'm afeard mine will come that way if the weather doesn't change."

"No, Eliza." Jared spoke quickly, and so sharply that Eliza held her head straight and was riveted by his tone. "No, never say that again. Never think that again. Your babe will have a warm welcome, something that's more than fire on a hearth or water boiling in a kettle. Haven't we made the room ready? Aren't we all waiting with hearts as eager as the birds for the dawn? Now, rest you awhile."

Eliza leaned back and closed her eyes. The wisp of a smile moved across her lips. "I'm so tired, Jared. It was hard coming up the hill from the valley, and the wind pierced me through–but here–there's warmth. I'm not afeard now, nor will I be when the time comes."

One by one and each in his own way, all the family turned to Jared during the terrible days of that Arctic winter whose grip over the land seemed so relentless, for there was warmth in his presence and strength in his words.

A few nights later, when the brown cow began her piteous mooing, Jared was asleep. John Dunklee, watching by the fire, went out to the barn to attend her. There was no sleep for the other animals that night, and no contented chewing of cud or munching of hay. Sheep, oxen, cows, horses, and fowl stared into the dank darkness so barely shattered by the light from Dunklee's tin lantern while the brown cow gave birth to a stillborn heifer.

Dunklee sighed. Up and down the country the farmers were losing their young stock during the bitter weather, and though it might put veal on the pantry shelves for a good time to come, it made the herd that much smaller. There were not enough cows anywhere these days for a farmer to stand the loss of a single one. Dunklee looked down at the limp, wet burden that the mother was licking. Her rough tongue was going over and over the fur with its pretty markings in a frenzied gesture impelled by instinct. Yet the old cow seemed to know as well as John Dunklee that the calf was dead.

Turning away, Dunklee took his lantern from a peg and went toward the house, thinking that he might as well leave the calf with its mother until morning, as the cow would be readier for a parting then. His heart felt heavy and his step matched it. Strange what there was about sorrow, he thought, that made a man feel old and very tired. He pulled off his boots in the kitchen, then went to Jared's cot and laid his hand on the thin shoulder. It was the time agreed on to change their watch.

Jared woke easily. "Is all well?" he asked.

"The calf has come," Dunklee answered, "but it's as dead as all the others around this countryside." He sighed and went over to his bed.

Jared pulled his boots on quickly and drew a coat over his heavy shirt. He looked to the fire and swung the crane with its kettle of water over the heat; then he went out to the barn.

The mother cow had ceased the frenzy of her licking and was drawing her tongue slowly over the calf. Jared went to her, talking softly all the time, and stroking between her curled horns. He gave her a measure of meal and, as she bent her nose to it, picked up the calf to bring it into the house. The cow made a quick move to follow him. Barred by her pen, she lowed a feeble farewell.

Jared laid the stiff creature on the warm bricks of the hearth. Moving quickly and as silently as a shadow in the room with its five sleeping people, he warmed cloths in the kettle of hot water and wrapped the calf in them. He fanned the fire to greater warmth and set a small pan of milk to heat; then he took the calf in his arms. He was only doing what

Mother Thaxter had said she had done for him when she had been called to take him away from beside the cold body of his mother.

"There wasn't much life in you, little Jared," she had told him, "but there was somewhat, and I had to make that somewhat feel it was wanted in the world. So I loved you as I loved my own, and I held you as close to my heart as I had ever held any of my own, and I prayed God that we might keep you with us, for I knew we needed you."

Jared could not remember having thought of those words since he was a little boy, but they came clearly to him now as he lay by the fire pressing the calf close to his body. In a voice so low that it would waken none of the sleepers, he talked to the calf. He prayed too, using the words he had learned from Mother Thaxter, who had first taught him about God, and the faith he had gained from Mr. Toppan.

The night wore on. Wind whistled about the house and snow driven before it stung at the windows. Cold crept over the floor, but there was a wide circle of warmth around the hearth into which no cold could enter. Just beyond the circle, just beyond the light of the fire but within its softly moving shadows, slept the Dunklee children in their trundle bed, and in the great bed John Dunklee–his face lined with weariness–and Eliza, her face sweet with peace.

A shred of light came weaving into the room. The black beyond the windows began to thin to gray. Jared dipped a wooden spoon in the milk that stood warm and ready near the ashes, and, pouring it into his palm, cupped his hand to the calf's mouth.

There was the slightest flickering of the calf's tail–so slight that it was almost none at all, like a breeze on a still summer day that is so quickly swallowed up in the stillness that it seems never to have been.

Then the tail flickered again and the nose pressed itself into Jared's palm. A faint sucking sound could be heard in the quietness of the room. Moments passed–moments that held the bliss of hours. Now there was no more milk in the pan by the ashes; a pile of damp cloths were moist on the bricks; a small imperious mooing came from the young calf trying to stand on unsteady legs, flicking its curl-tipped tail, while a deeper mooing echoed from the barn.

John Dunklee sat up in bed with a start. The small sound had wakened the other sleepers, too, with a sight to take the chill from the coldest morning. There was Jared Austin sitting cross-legged by the hearth, a smile as bright as a full moon on his face, and beside him was a five-hours-old heifer.

Tobit jumped up and down in the trundle bed for joy at a new living thing that had not been there when he went to bed.

"So, the brown cow's got her calf," Eliza said sensibly, then started to prepare the children for the day.

John Dunklee, sitting there on the edge of the bed, rubbed his eyes as if he could not believe what they saw.

Jared lifted the calf in his strong arms. "I'd best take the young one to the mother; she knows what's good for it," he said, and he left the room for the barn.

As the weeks went on, the nights remained cold, while the sun, rising higher, brought some moderation to the days, and people and animals began to accustom themselves more and more to the weather. Since the cold had to all appearances settled on them for the rest of the winter, the only thing to do was to get used to it. They were well into February now. The sun was strong, the days were lengthening, and with March there was bound to be thawing. The turn of the year was at hand when winter merged into spring. The struggle with the cold would soon have an end, and the struggle with the soil would soon have a beginning.

Now that spring was in sight, people could talk about the winter more readily, comparing experiences and relating adventures, and commencing to tell those tales which would be retold in chimney corners for years to come.

Some of the old-timers, whose memories reached far to the past even presumed to say that this winter did not compare to the so-called "Canada winter" of 1780, when for forty days there was neither rain nor thaw. One old man, who had been a boy twenty years before that winter, recalled the year of 1762 when snow lay six feet deep in all the woods and the temperature was many degrees below zero for weeks at a time.

There had been hard winters before in New England, and there would be hard winters again, but now that one more had been grappled with, there was not a family in the country that did not feel the stronger for it–no matter what their losses had been.

Jared had finished his work in the Dunklee house. Now, early every morning, he tramped the mile up the hill to Corban Cristy's. The hard-packed snow crunched underfoot, the wind whisked about him, and the sun sparkling on the white world studded it as with myriad diamonds. Near evening, when the light began to fail, Jared would leave his paints and brushes and tramp down the hill again to the cheer and friendliness of the Dunklee household, which was his accepted home. He had never been so happy in a task as he was in Corban Cristy's; indeed, his happiness grew and expanded with every task until he wondered how he would contain it.

Mr. Toppan had said that he must put himself into his work for the work to be lasting, and never had it seemed so easy for Jared to bring heart, body, and mind to bear on a task as it was in Corban Cristy's house. Jared was used to doing what people wanted. Here, where he had free scope, he was supplying ideas which, because they were so satisfying, seemed to be Cristy's own.

In the early evenings by the fire, when John Dunklee might be stitching shoes for the children or hammering out some needed wooden implement for the house, and Eliza's fingers were tirelessly busy with sewing or knitting, they would ask Jared about his work. But Jared could never tell them much. Until it was complete in his mind and thus complete on the bare walls, he could be coaxed to say only a little.

"Did the work go well today?" Eliza would ask, glancing up from the woolens on her lap.

"Yes, it went well," Jared would answer, looking dreamily at her and seeing the walls he was doing instead of the person he was addressing.

"You're wearing a smile these days the way you wear your jerkin–it's never off you," Eliza went on.

"I like the work," Jared replied. "I like to think of the lass Corban will bring there, come June. But you shall see the walls too, Eliza," he promised.

She smiled. Nothing could be more beautiful than the walls Jared had done for her, but she looked forward to seeing those he was doing for her neighbor.

"Someday soon, Jared," she said, "you'll be readying a house for a lass of your own."

Jared's eyes lost their dreamy gaze. "Someday I shall, and the day may not be so far off either."

"You have a lass in mind?"

Jared nodded, and his eyes were bright with happiness, soft with memory.

"Who is she, Jared?"

"Her father farms on the far side of yonder mountain. We were brother and sister together all our early years, and ever since I can remember I've loved her. I haven't seen her since I went off with Mr. Toppan."

"Why don't you see her, Jared, since she lives not a day's journey off?"

Jared hesitated, then with a curious gesture he held out his two hands before him–supple hands they were, and strong, with fine long fingers; knowing hands. "She's one that wants something fine from life. I've got naught to give her but what my hands can do. When they have worked well for me, I'll take the fruits to her."

Eliza put her sewing down and leaned toward Jared. "Go see her soon, Jared. A girl looks early for a husband in this country. Don't trust to waiting long."

Jared turned toward the fire. He could not tell Eliza all. He could not even say that when the time was right–when he felt within his heart brave enough to face his father–he would go for Jennet. Jennet, even as the little girl he knew best and remembered well, was so strong, so self-reliant, so full of courage that he knew he could not go to claim her until his heart was wholly free from fear; then he would be all of a man in his own right.

The days moved on toward spring, and Jared worked in the empty house, for Corban spent most of his time in the barn with the stock or in the woods felling trees and clearing brush for wider pastures. Jared kept a fire on the hearth of the room that would be the parlor, and near it he kept his paints and the brushes he was not using; to it he came to loosen his fingers when they became so stiff from the cold that they were no longer obedient to his mind. So happy, so interested was he in the work that he hardly sensed the cold around the walls of the room, until hands and feet making their demands made him conscious that such a thing as cold had to be reckoned with.

In the small entryway of the house, Jared hung a frieze of bells, but such bells as had never been hung before, delicate and light with dainty swags and tassels. Wedding bells, liberty bells, church bells they were, all in one, with their promise, their freedom, and their comfort. That was the upper frieze.

Above the wainscot was the pineapple, true to the countryside's tradition of hospitality, there where the eye of a caller would first see it. Then there were lesser and indeterminate designs framing the doors into the two rooms and color laid on them all with skill and judgment.

The walls pleased Jared as he surveyed them. They spoke of welcome and cheer. They had been difficult to do, for there was warmth of neither sun nor fire in the entryway, and wind had hurled itself against the door and found countless unseen ways of penetration. Jared had been glad then that he was thin, for there was less of him to counter the cold. But always his joy in his work was like a warm mantle around him, though it did not keep his paints from freezing.

When Jared finally brought Corban Cristy to see the entryway, the big man standing there–looking twice as big, so muffled up in woolens he was–let out a long, low exclamation of satisfaction.

"It's fit for a royal palace," he said, and admiration turned a wide smile across his face. "I don't know where such skill comes from, Jared Austin. It's uncanny. But I'm glad you've got it. Why, if I speak above a whisper those bells will start ringing!"

Jared smiled. "They are meant to do just that when you bring your bride across the threshold and never cease all the days you spend together here."

Corban nodded. "I've a good mind to fetch the lass to see the job."

"No, Corban," Jared said quickly; and because he knew there was no way to stop Corban Cristy's mind once it was set on something, he added, "not until the other room is done, too."

"When will that be?"

Jared thought ahead to the work to be done. "By mid-April I'll have it finished." He smiled and added more cautiously, "I think I'll have it done, and I generally do what I think I'll do."

"Mayhap I'll wait until then," Corban said doubtfully.

"It's bitter weather now to bring a lass on a long journey to see a few painted walls in a cold, bare house."

"She's strong. She won't mind the cold. She's as strong as a young ox."

"Of course she is," Jared said. "Any woman to be fit for you, Corban, would have to be strong and brave; but there's something about women–strong as they are, they like to be the objects of a little tender care. Life is hard enough for them. It's a good thing not to make it any harder."

Corban nodded. "That's sound enough, Jared Austin, and if I wait till April to fetch her–on a day when the sun is high and the birds are singing–it'll be better; I've plenty to do before then. Why, I've been kept so busy with tending the stock all winter that I've hardly begun to build the furniture yet!"

"I'll give a hand to you on that when you're ready," Jared said.

Corban laid his hand on Jared's shoulder in a clumsy gesture of appreciation. "Money can't pay you, Jared Austin, for the work you do when you come to a house."

"Maybe it can't." Jared smiled shyly up at the man towering above him. "But money in your pocket is a fine thing all the same."

When March wore into April, Jared left the Dunklees' and moved his few possessions up to Corban Cristy's so that he would have every available hour of daylight for his work. The Gray One neighed cheerfully as she was given a stall in the barn, and Young Meteor, Cristy's powerful stallion, neighed in response.

The spring sun coming into the parlor on which Jared was at work was high and strong, and it did more to warm the whole room than the fire on the hearth did. Jared's heart beat fast with joy as he placed his stencils on the walls–stencils of flowers just picked from the garden, quick with life, fragrant and beautiful; and because summer's wealth had been remembered in the white grip of such a winter as no one had known before, the flowers were fashioned with all the loving tenderness that memory could bestow.

Over the fireplace Jared laid his most daring design–two love birds holding from their beak a looped cord, and on the cord two hearts become one. It was the culmination of all his desire, of all his imagining of what a bride's house should contain. Traditional as it was to entwine red hearts some-where in the decoration, he had wanted to take only the semblance of tradition and bring it to the very perfection of feeling in this house where two lives would soon be united, and where two hearts–with all their mingled longings–must become one for their own good and the good of those who would come after. This, then, was the best he could do and had ever done. Jared knew it as he looked at the finished walls.

When he laid his tools down and crossed the room to sit on a little stool and survey his work, he wondered–quite apart from his usual crescendo of confidence–whether he could ever do another such task. He sighed. He was tired, and somehow felt drained of all thoughts and ideas. He would like to go and lie on a hillside and let the rain wash him clean and the sun dry him and the stars shed their light on him. He would like to be quiet for a long time; perhaps for a whole day from dawning to dawning, perhaps for a month of such days. Only then would he feel life stir within him again, ideas and the need to express them pricking him to activity. But now, all he could think of, all he could desire, was quiet.

He looked over at the brushes and stencils lying on the floor, at the paint pots with color dripping down their sides, and he wondered who would pick them up and put them away, for he felt without the strength to do it just then. He put his head in his hands. It was heavy, and his hands were rough and cold. It must be at such times, he thought, that a man looks to a woman. The touch of her hands would instill life again, for her whole being was so quick to give life.

Corban Cristy could be heard coming in from the barn, shaking the wet snow from his boots, crossing the kitchen, opening the door to the parlor. Standing on the threshold, he breathed deeply as he saw the finished room–the walls with their designs that were as gracious and free as swallows in flight. They were Cristy's walls now, for they had gone from Jared Austin through stencil and brush and had become his by right of purchase. Cristy sighed from a depth of wonder and delight; then he turned and saw Jared–a small, bent-over figure, like a reed broken in two.

"Man, are you ill?" Cristy exclaimed, anxiety almost over-ruled by inadequacy, for if Jared were, he knew not what he would do.

Jared shook his head and his whole body moved with the motion. "Just tired," he murmured.

Corban walked around the room, examining each detail in that perfection of design and execution which Jared had developed under Mr. Toppan. Nowhere was there a line that had wavered. Nowhere was there a brush stroke other than true.

"I shall fetch the lass tomorrow," Cristy said, and Jared nodded, though the words had little meaning to him.

After Corban left the room and twilight had deepened into night, Jared rose from the stool and picked up his stencils. There were still coals in the ash on the hearth, and one by one the stiff paint-covered papers were laid on them. The paper smouldered for a while, then burst into flame, and the flickering light illumined the stencils on the walls as the stencils themselves went down to ashes.

Jared slept that night as he had not slept as long as he could remember. When he awoke, Cristy was not there, and in the barn the stall was empty where Young Meteor had stood. There were tracks of a horse traveling swiftly in the softening ice and mud of the road.

The day was bright with sunshine, and the cold April wind was thinly clad with warmth. Jared cleaned his brushes, capped his paint pots, and set them in orderliness. He swept the rooms, leaving all in readiness for Corban and the lass. He did his chores with the numbness of one who could sum-mon the habit of strength without its will. Then he left the house and started across meadows still lying deep in snow.

Once he was in the woods, the land rose steeply and Jared began to breathe deeply as the cold air circled about him and the sun rested a warm hand on his back. A half mile back in the woods was the crest of a small hill and a clearing. The snow had melted and run off from the clearing, and the earth was damp and brown with a tinge of green fire running through the ground covering. Here was life and growth reaching out for the sun's warmth, and here was rest for Jared–not the rest of sleep but the rest that soothed his mind, laying it fallow for a season.

He stretched his lean body out on a fallen pine and lay looking up at the sky. He dreamed then, with wide open eyes and a smile on his face. What was his work if it did not grow better, clearer, nobler with each task, even as he prayed to grow each day?

"Yes, I've done good work and I shall do even better when next I take up my brush," he said aloud to the high blue vault above him. He said it over and over again, shouting the words, whispering them, gaining vigor with each utterance.

The sun had climbed to midday, and because Jared was ready to face the world again, he got up from the fallen tree and started down the hill and through the woods. The slope of the land and the new thoughts coursing through him gave speed to his feet, even through the deep-lying snow with its icy crust. Reaching the edge of the woods, he paused at the sound of voices–deep laughter entwined with high–coming up the road.

It was Corban with his lass riding pillion behind him. Young Meteor, for all his strength, was plodding heavily through the mud, his sides steaming from the hard work and long winter coat still unshed. They made a fair picture and, as they drew nearer, Jared smiled for delight at them. The stallion was a handsome creature, carrying himself so loftily, with a long switch tail that streamed out bravely in the wind, and Corban sat him with the ease of one who has perfect understanding with animals. His head was held high, his broad shoulders were squared like those of a knight of old who would fight in tourney for his lady and win for the love he bore her.

As they approached the barn where they would leave Young Meteor, Jared saw what a match for Corban the lass was; for she was a sturdy well-set up girl, as young and fresh as morning dew, with arms strong for work in house or field. She wore a blue dress under her coat, and her thick brown hair hung loose and windblown on her shoulders.

"Jennet Thaxter!" Jared cried aloud, and with joy in his being started to run from the woods toward her.

Then a wall rose up before him and stopped him, a wall of realization. This was not the Jennet he knew–lovely and memorable and possessed through the years–but the Jennet who was to be Corban Cristy's bride, come June. With a feeling of numbness around his heart, Jared moved back to the shelter of a tree, pressing himself against the roughly fissured bark of a maple big enough to hide him.

"Oh, Jennet–" he cried aloud in the strange, listening silence of the woods.

Twice during the time the two were in the house, Cristy came to the door and called loudly for Jared. The third time Jennet lifted her voice after his, lutelike and clear, calling the name she had called so often in her childhood. But Jared, nailed to the tree by an anguish he was trying to find the way to bear, made no answer.

They were approaching the barn and their voices came sharply on the wind.

"He was tired last night when he finished," Corban was saying; "like as not he's gone to the woods for a spell of rest."

"Couldn't we go and find him?" Jennet was asking, and it was still the voice of a little girl who was used to making her way alone.

"No, lass," Corban answered gently. "I promised your mother to have you home by nightfall, and if we go floundering through the snow in the woods, who knows when we'll get back?"

They were on Young Meteor now. Down the road. Down the hill. Moving slowly through the mud. Moving with the quick clop of willing hooves where the road was hard.

The sun was drawing shadowy lines over the snow. The wind had no longer even an edge of warmth. The mud in the road was freezing, and pools of water left by the sun were being sheeted with ice. Then a small frightened voice came crying out of the gathering twilight.

"Jared! Jared!"

Jared lifted his face from the rough press of the maple's bark and listened; then he peered out from around the tree trunk.

"Jared, where are you?"

It was Tobit, spattered with mud, breathless from the long run uphill.

Jared ran quickly across the field. He was beside the little boy, folding him in his arms.

The fright on Tobit's face melted into tears of relief at finding Jared, and for a moment he could say nothing but gulp his sorrow and gasp for breath.

"Mama's took bad," he sobbed. "No one is home–Papa and the others went to market–two days ago–I came for you."

"Oh!" Jared picked Tobit up in his arms and ran with him into the barn.

A few quick motions and the Gray One had a bridle flung over her head, a blanket tossed over her back. Jared led her outdoors and mounted lightly; then he drew Tobit up in front of him. They were hurrying down the road, through mud and ice into the fast-falling night.

Chapter Seven

As they approached the Dunklee house, Jared saw with a catch in his heart that there was no light in any window. It was the first time of all the many nights he had drawn near that house that a beam of light had not reached out its friendly gleam to guide him in. They swung into the barnyard, and Jared left the Gray One for Tobit to tend; then he hurried to the house. There was a low, frightening sound issuing from the small room off the kitchen.

"I'm coming, Eliza," Jared called through the darkness. He groped his way across the kitchen to the hearth, where he reached for a coal to light a candle with; then he hurried in to Eliza, holding the candle high above him.

He almost did not recognize her, for her face was strangely contorted–not only with pain but with fear. He grasped one of her hands and held it tightly for a moment before he spoke.

"Shall I go for Nancy Preston?"

"No, no–oh, Jared–there isn't time," she gasped between breaths. "Don't leave me." The grip of her fingers closing around his hand was like a vise.

"But Eliza, I–" Jared began; then he knelt down on the floor by her bed. Setting his candle on a table, he stroked her forehead, hoping that the touch of a hand, clumsy though it might be, would loose the cordon of fear that was binding her.

"Listen to me, Eliza," he bade in a strange tone that for all its tenderness was so stern with compulsion that it drew her gaze to him and held it fast. "You must tell me what to do so I can help you, but I will do it only if you will obey me. Ease yourself and open your eyes wide. Look at the roses we planted on these walls."

She loosed her grip on his hand and some of the tenseness passed from her body. Her lips cast off their taut grimace and found their old way of smiling, wan though the smile was.

"Stay with me, Jared. I won't fear then," she whispered.

"No, you need not fear; have faith," Jared said quietly. "See that rose, Eliza, that the candle is shedding its light on? When it bloomed, it opened its petals to sun and rain, wind and night, and it was cared for through them all. Do you think God would care for the rose and not for you?"

She clutched his hand again as a spasm of pain shot through her. "Jared." Her words came as if there were no voice behind them, only a hard whistling breath. "I must say something to you now."

"Not now, Eliza, don't trouble yourself so; a little later will do."

"Later may be too late–for me." She struggled for breath as a swimmer might for air against an overwhelming wave. "Go for her soon–claim the thing you love. Promise me you will, Jared." She gripped his hand.

Jared looked away into the shadows of the room, knowing he would never go over the mountain now after Jennet; but how should he tell Eliza that, when at this moment her peace seemed to depend upon his promise?

"Eliza," he said, "could I talk to you of faith if it were not in my own heart?"

A smile quivered on her lips, and the grip she had laid on Jared's hand relaxed.

Tobit could be heard coming through the passage from the barn. Jared went to the door of the kitchen. Tobit was standing there, his eyes smeared with tears, bewilderment on his face.

"Jared, you won't let Mama die, will you?"

Jared smiled at him. "No, Tobit, but I've more work than my two hands can do. Will you help me?"

Tobit nodded quickly. To be able to do some task–no matter what it might be that Jared would ask of him–was to shake off the thing that had been clutching him by the throat.

"Get more life in the fire, Tobit," Jared said. "Let it flame and crackle as you would on the coldest night. Fill the pot with spring water and swing it over the flame. Stay beside it until I call you."

"Yes, Jared," Tobit answered, then ran with all the speed of eager feet to do his tasks.

He fetched water from the spring and filled the iron kettle; then he blew the coals into leaping flames and put sticks on them until the water was boiling. He stood watching the water as it slowly began to steam. Then, after a long time, it started swirling in the kettle and Tobit gazed on, fascinated by the movement of the boiling water. Suddenly he was startled by a cry from the room that had roses on its walls. He pricked up his ears. It was a new sound, a sound he had never heard before. The cry came again. Then Tobit knew that it was a voice, and a smile spread over his tear-streaked face.

Jared came from the room toward the circle of light cast by the fire. In his arms he carried something small and lively.

"Fetch a basin, Tobit, and let us see how well your brother can swim."

On the hearth they set a basin and made the water right; then Jared washed the babe who squirmed and wriggled like a slippery fish. Tobit watched with eyes that blinked in tenderness and wonder.

"May I touch him, Jared?"

"You may do more than that, Tobit; you may hold him for me," Jared said, drying the babe. He wrapped him in a soft woolen blanket that had come from Eliza's loom that winter and now smelt sweetly of rose leaves and lavender from the oak chest. "Sit down and take him in your arms, so, while I go to your mother."

Tobit sat still, holding the babe in arms that quivered with joy, crooning softly to it. The child, turning its puckered red face from side to side, seemed to hearken to the little boy's words as Tobit poured out his love upon him.

Marveling to himself at what had taken place, Tobit contemplated the babe long and happily. Only a short time ago he had thought something terrible had happened to his mother, yet when Jared had come back to the dark house with him, it had not proved terrible at all but wonderful; for where there had been crying there was now quiet, and where he had been alone with his mother, now he was not alone, but with his little brother.

Jared came back to the hearth and took the babe from Tobit.

"Come, Tobit," he said, "we'll go in and see your mother now."

With gentle steps they crossed the threshold of the borning room. Tobit knew instinctively that here the thing that was so wonderful had happened. What it was he did not know, but he was hushed before it. Jared had set more candles in the room, and it was full of a warm glow lighting the pink of the roses and the strong green stems uplifting them.

Eliza was smiling, lying there and holding out one arm to cradle the babe and the other to put around Tobit; and her eyes were as soft as shadows on a summer's night.

"Tobit," Jared was saying, "stay here now and do whatever your mother wants, and leave her only long enough to keep the fire blazing on the hearth."

"Oh, Jared, I am so warm–so happy." Eliza smiled up at him. "Think of it, another boy to help John in the fields! But you're not leaving us?"

"Yes, Eliza, I must hasten to the village to see if John is back and give him the news. 'Twill help speed him to you. You're in good hands."

Tobit looked at Jared proudly. His was the task of protection on this first of all nights that his brother was spending in the world.

Jared patted him on the shoulder and then went quietly from the room to the barn, where the Gray One neighed in the darkness and guided Jared to her. She nuzzled her nose along his shoulder, and just for a moment Jared leaned his head against her fine strong neck. The ache in his heart had come back again now that the moment's urgent needs had been met. He sighed, then tossed the blanket over the sturdy back and led her out the door and into the frosty silence of the night.

The mud had frozen and the ruts in the road made the going slow. The Gray One chose her way well and, responding to her master's wish, quickened her pace whenever the road gave her a chance to do so. But it was a long journey, and during it Jared had time to think things out. Eliza's words kept ringing in his ears. *"Claim the thing you love."* Strange that the bright flame of a woman's intuition so far outshone the hard metallic light of a man's reason. Jared saw now that had he been quick and brave enough to claim Jennet, he might have had her all this past year. Living with the memory of her, as he had been doing for so long, he had been defrauding himself. What odd justice lay in the fact that the house he had put his best into was to be her house!

The hurt in his heart felt as sharp as a knife wound, yet his eyes were seeing farther than they had ever seen before. Sight was one thing and with it a man saw what the eye beheld; but vision was something more: with it a man saw what the eye could never see. Pain was the opening of a door; through it birth came, and through it man grew up.

But must all growth come through pain? Jared asked himself, finding the answer in another question. Would he have known this pain if he had gone over the mountain months ago and talked to Jennet as a man could talk once in his life to the woman he loved? He had not gone over the mountain, for he had feared to face his father; and he had been so sure that Jennet would wait. If he had been fearless, if he had done the thing he had known all along he should do, he would not be experiencing such pain now. That was the answer then.

It was a night for the stars to bless with light–for Eliza, who through the travail of her body had given a child to the world, and for Jared, who through the travail of his soul was giving a man to the world.

A new life was opening before him, a life without Jennet. At first it seemed huge and bare and lonely, for he had lived with the thought of her as long as he could remember. But now Jared knew that never again would he feel the whistling wind of fear; never again would he shiver before it. This very night he had reminded Eliza of God's faithfulness; he could trust Him for the years that lay ahead.

Jared looked up to the stars and felt such strength as brought light to his mind and a smile to his lips: not the brave smile of a man who fronts despair with a mask of cheer, but the trusting smile of a man who breaks the sword of will in two and casts the fragments away. Young as he was, Jared knew that he had been born to manhood.

The lights of the village houses were streaming out on the night, and the Gray One quickened her pace. Jared drew up to the inn and left the mare standing by the steps. There was light and noise within and the sound of heavy voices in argument and talk. Jared pushed the door open quickly and stood in its shadow, his eyes confused for a moment by the light. A dozen heads near the fire turned to see who the newcomer was, and a dozen voices fell to nothing. There was a silence like that following the sermon on a Sunday morning. Then the heads turned back to the fire.

"John Dunklee," Jared called out, amazed by the strange chill in the warmth of the inn. "I have a message for you from your wife."

John Dunklee rose from the circle by the fire and came toward Jared. His face looked hard, and as he spoke, his eyes did not meet those of Jared.

"Speak it, then," he said.

"The babe has come." Jared announced the news quietly. "And another son you have, John Dunklee."

John looked up quickly and stepped forward, laying a hand on Jared's arm. "And Eliza–is she all right? Did Nancy Preston get there in good time?"

Jared smiled. "She's all right, John, and happy as a songbird with the babe in her arms and Tobit beside her to do whatever she may want. There is no one else. But she wants you, John."

John was already buttoning his coat. "My horses are tuckered from the journey, and the wagon is loaded heavy."

"The Gray One stands outside," Jared said. "Take her, and I'll come along with the wagon and the children."

"Thank you, Jared." John hurried out the door and almost instantly the quick traveling of a horse could be heard making its way on the rutted road.

Jared turned and moved toward the fire. The circle of men parted and made a space for him, saying nothing. Jared held out his hands to the blaze.

"It's cold for mid-April," he commented.

There was no reply. When Jared's hands were warm, he looked toward the two Dunklee children who were sitting close together in a corner of the fireplace.

"Come Delight, come Reuben; we must be after your father on the way home."

They got up from their places and followed him to the door. While they were lacing their boots and fastening their cloaks, Dan True came over to Jared.

"I hear you've finished Corban Cristy's house," he began.

"Yes, it is finished," Jared replied eagerly, "and I'm ready now to do your walls if you're still minded."

Dan shook his head slowly. "I'm not minded. I'm not going to do my walls this spring; so perhaps you'd best be looking for work elsewhere."

"I shan't go elsewhere till summer. I've promised to help Corban make his furniture."

Dan True lowered his voice and put his hand on Jared's shoulder. "If you knew what was good for you, Jared Austin, you'd go elsewhere for a time." He smiled awkwardly, then shrugged his shoulders and, raising his voice, bade Jared good-night.

"Thank you, Dan," Jared said, opening the door.

The children started ahead, running toward the barn where the heavily loaded wagon stood. Jared followed, walking slowly in bewilderment.

The men grouped about the fire were known to him, yet they had shunned him, not as a stranger, but as the plague. True, they were for the most part men who had suffered through the terrible cold of the winter. Ephraim Twiss had lost all his stock one night; the wind had blown out a side of his barn and he had not known it until morning. Another had lost a newborn child. Another had not wood enough to carry him through the winter and had to go to the inn for warmth. As Jared thought of them, he knew that the whole countryside had suffered too. John Dunklee had kept stock and children alive, but it had not been easy, as Jared could have told anyone. Corban Cristy had fared well, but his place was still small and he had the strength of two men.

Jared reached the barn and with Reuben's help swung the harness over the broad backs of the team and fastened them to the wagon. The children climbed up on the seat; then Jared climbed up too and tucked the blankets around them. He took the reins in his hands. Slowly, heavily, the team plodded out of the inn yard and onto the road. Their thickly shod feet cared nothing for the ruts as they moved at one pace only–a deliberate walk.

Two days ago John Dunklee had gone to market, taking Reuben and Delight with him. Dressed hogs and poultry, cheeses and butter, apples, and some of Eliza's woolens had been traded or sold for sugar, flour, molasses, salt fish, and grain for the spring planting. There were supplies for months to come in the well-packed wagon that creaked noisily over the road.

Delight looked up at the stars and breathed happily; then she snuggled her head against Jared's shoulder. "Oh, Jared, I'm so glad you came. Those men were saying such silly things, and when you came they stopped."

She nodded to her brother. "You'd better tell him, Reuben. Begin at the beginning, and if you forget anything I'll remember it."

"Well," Reuben began, "about midafternoon we got back from market and stopped at the inn. The horses were mighty tired and Father said we all could do with some dinner."

"It was salt beef and Indian pudding," Delight put in, "and ginger water and bannock baked on a maple chip by the fire."

"There were lots of other people there," Reuben went on, "and then Mr. Corban Cristy came to the door with a young lady–"

"She was pretty, Jared," Delight added quickly, "and her cheeks were as red as the roses you painted on Mama's walls, and her hair was all tossed by the wind."

Reuben picked up the narrative after his sister's interruption. "Then while Mr. True was giving them supper, Mr. Cristy told everyone what wonderful walls you had made for him in his house, and the young lady said she used to know you when you were a little boy–like me."

Jared nodded. "Yes, we grew up together, just like you and Delight."

"She said–" then Reuben stopped.

"Go on," Jared urged kindly.

"I–I don't want to."

"You must always finish what you have begun, Reuben."

Reuben swallowed hard; then he began again. "She said that when you were born all the apples were killed, and your mother died too–that it was cold as it has been this past winter–and that now you have come back to these parts, it is cold again."

Jared felt the night wind around him as if he were in a house with all its windows suddenly opened. "And then?" he asked, trying to keep his voice steady.

"Then–" Reuben breathed more easily since the worst was over. "Then the young lady and Mr. Cristy went off riding over the mountain and everybody began to talk–and they didn't stop until you came in the door."

"What did they say?" Jared felt that his voice was coming from far away.

"Lots of things. They said you had brought the cold with you, and that you were the Devil."

Delight laughed as if it were a good joke. "Even I could have told them that the Devil comes from a hot place! That shows how silly they were."

"You won't go away, will you, Jared?" Reuben pleaded.

"Why should I go away?"

"Everyone said you should. They said you'd be better off."

"No," Jared answered, and his voice was firm and strong. "I won't go away. I have work to finish here, and a man can't look for more work until he finishes what he has got at hand." So that was what Dan True meant, Jared thought, as he recalled the innkeeper's kindly pleading.

Delight started humming to herself a song she had learned by her mother's spinning wheel; then she broke into the words and Reuben joined her in the chorus:

> *"There was a little woman*
> *As I've heard tell,*
> *Fol-lol, did-dle, did-dle, dol,*
> *She went to market her eggs to sell,*

Fol-dol, did-dle, did-dle, dol,
She went to market all on a market day,
And she fell asleep all on the King's highway,
Fol de rol de lol lol, lol lol lol,
Fol, lol, did-dle, dol."

Their voices were high and merry on the night, louder than the creaking of the wagon wheels. They were rounding the bend and the horses were pulling harder, as if they knew that their own warm barn was near. Lights were shining from the house. Smoke rising from the chimney lifted itself high and swung like a plume in the air. Jared stopped at the door to let the children down.

"Go and greet your new brother; I'll be in after the horses are bedded."

With shouts of glee, Reuben and Delight ran into the house. Jared backed the wagon into a covered shed, then undid the traces and led the horses into the barn. They had had a long day's hard pulling and, for all their ponderous strength, were weary. Jared rubbed them down well and mixed mash for them, thinking that it was well the days of outdoor pasturage were at hand, as the meal was getting low.

He stroked their great heads as they bent over their mangers and talked to them in a way he felt they understood; then he went over to the Gray One to see to her. She had grown wise during the years they had been itinerating together, and there were times when Jared liked to turn to her for counsel. She whinnied as he came into her stall, lifting her velvet nose from the hay to rest it on Jared's shoulder.

Footsteps could be heard coming from the house. Streaks of light from a tin lantern preceded John Dunklee's entrance into the barn.

"Jared?" he called, holding the lantern above his head.

"Here I am." Jared stepped out of the shadow of his mare into the circle of light.

John Dunklee drew nearer; then he put his hand on Jared's shoulder. "Thank you, Jared, for all you have done for Eliza this night. I–" He hesitated. Gratitude was in his heart, but the expression of it came awkwardly to his tongue.

Jared's smile gave a light to his face in the darkness of the barn. "Say naught about it, John. It was little enough that I could do."

"And Jared, I'm shamed–" John hung his head for a moment, then lifted it and faced the younger man squarely. "I want to say I'm sorry for speaking to you the way I did at Dan True's. I'll stand by you, Jared, after what you've done this night, no matter what happens–and you've always got a home with us, remember that."

"John, I don't understand what this means. The children prattled about something on the way home, but it made small sense to me."

"It means, Jared, that a few of the folk around here are against you."

"But I've done nothing wrong."

"There's been a lot of suffering this cold winter, and they're trying to find somewhere to lay the blame. You were handy. And they've had too much time to sit around and gossip."

"But weather's weather, John. Man has naught to do with it but make the best of what comes to him. Did it all start with what Corban's lass said? She meant no harm, I'm sure of that."

"She meant no harm, but she made it all the same. She told of the cold that came when you were a babe, and how she'd heard there was no cold like it in all these years since. When she and Corban left, the men started talking."

"And drinking too, I'll wager."

"Yes, there was rum nearby to warm their blood and twist their minds. They said there had never been such a winter– and then they got to saying how the weather turned when you came here. And then–"

"Well, what then, John?" Jared felt like a schoolteacher prompting the recital of a lesson.

"Then they tried putting two and two together. They said the skill you had with a brush couldn't possibly be your own but must come from the dark place."

Jared smiled and shook his head.

Reluctantly, Dunklee added, "They said it was an odd thing your not feeling the cold as most folks did–'twasn't natural."

Jared smiled again. "And what else, John? I'm learning many things about myself."

"I had told them one time how you cosseted my calf to life and they brought that up–said that only a man with inhuman powers could do such a thing."

"John, there was life in the calf. It needed only to be awakened." Jared shook his head again. "Sounds like it was the rum speaking."

"Rum or no, it's bad business when men get to talking that way, seeing things that way." John Dunklee sighed, and then he went on. "I'm worried, Jared. Folks used to be tried for witchcraft–and hung too–on far less score than these men have against you."

"Not in New Hampshire," Jared replied stoutly. "And not in all of New England for a hundred years or more."

"True," John agreed, "but madness, once aroused, is hard to stop. You ought to go away, Jared."

"Go away–and leave a lie hanging in midair?" Jared shook his head. "No, John, I'll stay until every man takes back his words. But I'll not bring harm to this house. I'll go on living up at Corban's, if he'll have me, and if he won't, I'll live in the woods."

Jared turned to lead the Gray One from her stall.

"You're not leaving now?" But for all the kindness in John's question, there was relief too.

Jared nodded. "Yes, Eliza's most likely asleep, and the children will soonest forget what they've heard if I'm not around to remind them of it."

"Have you had any supper?" John asked, eager to do something.

"Supper?" Jared's mind hurtled back over the day that had begun so long ago—that had seen him in the high clearing, by the rough trunk of the maple, at Eliza's bedside, on the dark road, at the inn, and now in the barn. He'd had bread and cheese that morning, but it seemed an age had passed since then.

He shook his head. "I'm not hungry, John, thank you."

The lines around John's lips curved up and his eyes twinkled. "That's the sort of thing men hold against you. Feeling hunger is natural, just like feeling cold."

"When a man can eat, it's good to be hungry; when he can't, it's better to forget the taste of food," Jared said briefly.

The Gray One was bridled and blanketed again and led out into the night. The two men stood together by the barn door for a moment; the light of the lantern dimmed by the twinkling of a sky of stars. They grasped hands.

"I'll be true to you, Jared, come whatever may."

"I know you will, John, and I thank you for it. Good-bye."

Jared mounted the mare and took the reins in his hands, pointing her head up the mile-long climb to Corban Cristy's. And there was an odd lightness in his heart which the Gray One responded to as she picked her way quickly and skillfully over the frozen ridges in the road.

Chapter Eight

Corban did not get back until noon the next day, and since he had stopped at Dan True's for a meal, he knew the talk that was going around the village about Jared.

"But I told them all they were as mad as witch hunters," he said heartily to Jared, "and that if they so much as laid a finger on you I'd string each one from his own ridgepole!"

Jared laughed. "That's a big order, Corban. I hope you won't have to take it on."

The plain, blunt honesty in Corban's face was good to look upon. Here was a man of will and muscle whose mind was as unbending as a granite boulder and as clean as the wind that blew across his fields; a man who relished what he understood and whose talk was the language of strong hands. What he did not understand–superstition and the like–he would have nothing to do with.

"I told them they were a parcel of fools and not fit to put plow to New Hampshire earth," Corban went on. "True it is that it's been a bad winter, but planting time is near and growing weather, then harvest. They'll forget their foolishness when once they get to work on the land. They've been sitting around hearths so long that they can't do aught better than gossip like a lot of old women. Your home is right here, Jared Austin. We'll get the furniture made, and I'll be glad to have you help me with the planting, but–" he hesitated, looking at Jared warily.

"What is it, Corban?"

"You're scrawny to do much heavy work."

"I'm strong enough," Jared said with a laugh. Then he looked away from Corban for a moment. "You're getting married in June?"

Corban nodded. "June's a good time for a wedding, but if I'm too busy with the land, the lass will have to wait till harvest is over." He sighed, "I'm that sorry, Jared, that you didn't see the lass. She said she used to know you well, that you grew up together."

"We were brother and sister," Jared replied, and the saying was easier than he had thought it would be.

"She's that pleased with the walls that you'd think she'd ordered them herself–and I never told her I was having them in the house!" Corban beamed with pride.

Jared smiled. "I'm pleased at that."

So the two men went ahead getting ready for the spring planting. The seeds stood in their sacks by the barn door. The potatoes were sprouting in the cellar, so ready were they for the ground. The plow was in readiness. The horses were strong and fat from their easy winter in the barn. Everything was at hand but the weather.

"The season is late this year," Corban said briefly as April came to a close. The ground was hard with frost; snow still lay deep on northerly slopes, and the ponds were gray with rotting ice.

"The frost is out of the ground in the high clearing," Jared remarked, fitting together the joints of a table he was working on. "I went up there yesterday, and the ground was soft and moist. We could plow that piece and get it planted."

Corban laughed loudly. "What's up there–an acre or two! 'Tisn't worth it, Jared."

"An acre of seed can give a pile of grain," Jared said quietly.

"Catch two fleas at one nip has always been my go-by," Corban answered. "When I put seed in the ground I like to put it where I can see it grow and where folks going along the road can see it, too." His tone had a finality that ruled out further discussion.

The month of May came in with sharp winds. There was no plowing to be done yet and–what was of even more immediate concern–the vegetation was so backward that there was no pasturage for the stock. Many people, not expecting a hard winter, had sold more of their hay in the autumn than was wise, and they were hard pressed for fodder. Others were salting their remaining hay and mixing it with potatoes in the endeavor to eke out food for their stock. Grimly it was realized, as tales came trickling in from travelers and peddlers traversing the country, that the strange conditions were not peculiar to New Hampshire, but prevailed throughout all New England.

However, by mid-May, warmth blew over the land, rain fell, and the frost began to ease itself out of the ground.

"We'll plow tomorrow and plant the day after," Corban said gleefully. "I heard a bobolink down in the meadow this morning, and the oak leaves are as large as a mouse's ear. We won't be so far behind time after all."

Jared shook his head. "This warmth's not come to stay. There's too much cold around here still. Wait a week, Corban, and see what happens."

"I'll wait for no man, Jared Austin, and I'll plant when the south wind is blowing. If you don't want to help me, you need not."

That night Jared walked down the muddy road, past the softening fields, to the Dunklees'. The children embraced him with glee. John and Eliza were warm in their greeting, and Eliza was quick to show him the babe in its cradle on the hearth–a bright babe with keen, searching eyes.

They had supper together. Afterward, when they were sitting around the long table, John said slowly, "I plowed today and I've half a mind to plant tomorrow."

"What does the other half of your mind say?" Jared asked.

"Wait and see what this south wind will do. It may shift north, like as not, and bring the cold back again."

"I want him to wait," Eliza said. "Time lost can be regained; seed lost makes us that much poorer."

"That's the better half speaking," Jared said with a smile.

Corban planted his fields during the next few days, coming in at noon and in the evening exceedingly pleased with himself. Jared stayed at his carpentry. He would not do what he could not see was right; so he said nothing to anyone and went on with the work of his hands. Flushed with pride and the feeling that he had put the bad weather in his pocket, Corban rode down to the inn in the evenings and talked with other farmers who had been doing their planting. They laughed together, for the weather had broken at last, and one and all felt sure that they had the jump on their more cautious neighbors.

In little more than a week, the corn was showing above the dark earth–thin spears that were tender and green and full of promise. The farmers who had waited awhile to plant were the laughingstock of the countryside. The rye had begun to show, too, and the barley. When another week had passed, Corban could look on his fields and see a haze of green running over the earth.

Not only was the seed prospering, but the grassland had commenced to grow. Cattle and sheep could be turned out into their pastures at last. Horses and colts were kicking up their heels at the freedom of open fields. Sheep were pressing quivering noses to the greening meadows. Cows seemed content to stand in the sun, meditatively chewing fresh grass.

The month was nearing its fourth week when the wind shifted and blew from the northwest. Cows and horses and sheep were brought in from the fields that night, and a backlog like that used in midwinter found its place on most hearths. In the white farmhouse on the hill, Corban Cristy paced up and down the kitchen most of the night. But not the will of man, nor his anger, nor the oaths that lips gave utterance to, could change the course of the weather.

Morning dawned cold and sparkling. The fields were covered with rime and the newly leafed trees and budding blossoms were hung with white. Jared watched the sun come up. It's beautiful, he thought, as the crystallized world responded to the light with glittering reflections. On the distant hills a blanket of snow was laid lightly, like a screen to gather up the rainbow of color carried with the sun. Then Jared looked at the fields. There was not a green blade standing above the frozen earth.

Corban said nothing to Jared when they faced each other over their breakfast, but his eyes looked like field stones on a winter day, and his lips were set in a hard line. After their meal, he went to his store room to measure out new sacks of seed, for he had not spent it all on the first planting. But there were farmers who had, and for them, that morning with its star-tipped, frosty beauty spelled only one thing: starvation for stock and family.

Jared went up through the woods to the high clearing. The frost had laid on the earth but not enough to kill. Seed planted there a fortnight ago would have been waving its green banners in this morning's wind, for the trees around the clearing gave shelter and protected the land.

At noon, Jared asked Corban to plow in the clearing and plant some seed there.

Corban looked at him as if he scarcely saw him. "And grow grain for the creatures of the woods to eat?" He shook his head and laughed coarsely.

Jared breathed deep. "Then may I plant there?"

"You?" Corban stared at him. "If you're that crazy. But not with my seed."

"I have a bag of seed of my own," Jared said, "payment on some work done last October."

Corban nodded, hearing little of what Jared said and caring less.

The first few days of June brought such warm rains and healing sunshine that the farmers who had not yet planted hastened to make up for lost time, and those who had planted and lost made their ground ready again. John Dunklee was one who put his seed in the ground that week. Reuben and Delight, with smaller bags over their shoulders, worked beside him, and on the sloping hillside Eliza set the seed potatoes in the warm earth. Tobit helped her; and the babe, swinging in a small cradle from the boughs of an apple tree, crowed to himself at the glory of the day. Corban Cristy strode up and down his fields, tossing the grain freely and singing to the wind, for he had seed to spare, even enough to sell to some less fortunate farmers, and he was pleased with his rolling land. The sun that day was enough to pale the memory of misfortune with its warm rays of assurance.

Jared took the Gray One up to the clearing and started to plow the land. The Gray One had never bent herself to field labor. When she struck a boulder she would become obstinate and balky, and there were boulders in plenty, and twisted roots, and now and then a stump as obdurate as granite. But the earth was good: virgin soil to which during the weeks of waiting Jared had brought muck from the swamp at the wood's edge. Mud was money to a farmer, and Jared had begun to see that nothing could be good enough for the clearing which Corban had said he might call his own.

By midafternoon the Gray One stood with her sides heaving, sweat dripping from her, and lather where the collar had rubbed. Jared leaned against a tree, ready to drop with weariness but determined to finish the plowing before nightfall. Then a laugh rang across the clearing—an odd sound on the still air that had known no other sounds than the turning of earth, the shriek when the plow shard struck a rock, and the heavy panting of man and horse.

Jared looked up. Corban stood across the clearing, one hand laid lightly against a tree trunk. He had finished his work and with the freedom a man feels when his work is done while others are still toiling, he had come up to watch Jared.

"You're crazy, Jared Austin," he called with a laugh,"–plumb crazy to think you can make this land fit for grain." Then with a dozen long strides he had crossed the rough furrows and was standing beside Jared. "Howbeit, hard work is a good kind of craziness."

Jared started to speak, but the weariness in him found words long in coming.

Corban had picked up the reins that lay over the handle of the plow. "I'll do a mite for you. Come on, girl," he bellowed.

The Gray One pulled together her heaving sides and bent to the plow, responding to Corban's knowing hand as she had not all day to Jared's; for Corban seemed to sense rocks and would veer to the left or right so they were not struck, and he had a feeling for the depth of the plow in the earth so the mare found the strain less. Long before sunset the field was finished and lay fallow to the coming night.

The two men walked down the path through the woods, the mare following slowly behind them.

"Planting tomorrow?" Corban asked.

Jared shook his head. "The land will do better if it lies open for a few days, and there's still harrowing to be done. I'll plant next week."

Corban nodded his head. "Have it your own way with your own land. My seed is all in again and will be sprouting soon these fine days."

"You were fortunate to have so much seed," Jared said.

Corban smiled. "A good granary and a good woodpile; add them together and they make a good husband, just as sure as adding two and two makes four." The work of the day and the accomplishment gave Corban a sense of well-being that could surmount the past.

"Hard times come often for a farmer," he went on, "but they go too. You have to take the rough with the smooth in this life."

Before the end of the first week in June, the cold came on again with high winds and the ground freezing at night, and it held for more than a week. Many a farmer saw his beans and tender plants that had been coming along nicely cut to the ground as if a sword had run over the earth. On some southerly slopes the grain was weathering the cold, but the Indian corn–such a mainstay for man and beast and fowl–was scarcely fit to hill up, no less weed, and the potato sprouts were measly.

Jared waited until the twenty-first of the month; then, on that longest day of the year, with the weather moderating, he trudged up to the clearing. Over his shoulder was slung the bag of seed Squire Tallant had given him. To Jared it had now become more meaningful than a bag of gold. As seed it might not be much, but as grain–what had Squire Tallant said? Something about having enough to feed a county if he used it well. God helping him, he would use it as well as he had ever used brushes on walls.

The ground in the clearing was soft and mellow, as if it had not frozen up during the recent cold spells. Jared pushed a lump with his foot and it crumbled before him. Then, with the fine fingers that had made flowers and trees of all kinds bloom under them, he tossed the seed into the air. Up and down the clearing he paced, while the seed fell to the ground and the earth took it to itself. The empty bag in his hand, Jared knelt down at the edge of the field.

"Oh, Father," he prayed aloud, "bless this seed as Thou hast blessed the work of my hands during many years. Let it grow green and strong and golden with harvest that Thy children may be fed. Oh, Father, may the creatures of the woodland see it with reverence and if they hunger let them have a little, but let most of it be for Thy children."

Then he rose and went down the hill through the woods and back to the house.

Corban was riding up the road and two empty bags were swinging from his saddle. Jared met him at the barn door.

"There's not a man around here will sell a single seed," Corban exclaimed, pointing to the empty bags. "What will this countryside do next winter?"

"What news is there at the inn?" Jared asked.

"The same everywhere," Corban answered. "Up and down New England, two plantings have been killed, and most of the seed is gone. Prices are so high in York state that no one can buy seed, even had he the heart. There won't be a loaf of bread on a single table this winter."

"But there'll be potatoes," Jared reminded him.

Corban nodded. "Maybe; small potatoes and few in a hill."

"Any further news?"

"Bad news. As if starvation weren't enough, there's sickness. In the West, the spotted fever has struck some villages; but you can't find out where it is, as there isn't a peddler will go near it."

They turned slowly and went into the house. Jared wanted to ask Corban about his marriage, since June was more than half gone, but the man had more on his mind than a wedding and his wrath broke easily. Hard luck had made him touchy.

The rooms were furnished now–plain wooden table and chairs, and a wooden bed simply but strongly made with a turning here and a bit of carving there to break the severity of its lines. There was no color or grace in the house; that would come with the woman when her hand wove bright woolens and coverlets, and her fingers set out pewter plates with their soft gleam, and china with its delicate light. Only the walls brought a measure of beauty, and Jared looked on them gratefully during these days of strain. The hearts and bells and the twining flowers pleased him and brought a smile to his lips, but Corban walked past them now as if he did not see them.

It was a small meal they had that night, for with the prospect of scant food for months to come it was best to be sparing with what was at hand.

Corban helped himself to more cheese. "It's a terrible thing to have a hole in you that's always empty," he said.

Jared looked across the table at the big man whose clothes had already begun to hang loosely on him. "I've often been glad the Lord made me thin," he said with a quiet chuckle. "When I was a little shaver and my father used to beat me, there wasn't so much of me to feel the rod. When the weather was cold, there wasn't so much of me to cover up."

Corban put his head in his hands. "Man, how can you laugh during times like these! My heart is so heavy within me that I'd be afeard to go near water, for I'd drown as sure as if I had a millstone tied around my neck."

He raised his head quickly. "Did you hear that knocking at the door?"

Jared nodded.

They listened again. It was not the bold sound a man makes when he seeks company, or the urgent sound a woman stirs when she's after help; but a light, questioning knock.

"Someone's wanting shelter," Jared said, rising quickly.

" 'Tis a woman, too," Corban muttered, striding across the room to the door. He flung it wide open so that the light of the room might shine on whoever stood on the doorstone.

"Jennet!" he exclaimed.

Jared came hastily to the door. "Jennet Thaxter!" he cried aloud, joy in his voice.

Jennet saw them both, and then, wide-eyed and travel-stained, dropped down on the doorstone and started weeping. A bundle she had been carrying slipped from her hands and rolled onto the grass.

Corban stood dumbfounded at such a visitor and such behavior, but Jared knelt down on the doorstone beside Jennet and started to help her up.

"She's near spent, Corban; give a hand that we may bring her in, then fetch a noggin of milk."

They brought her into the kitchen and set her in a chair. Corban brought some milk and offered it to her. She pressed it to her lips and drank eagerly. Then she looked up at him.

"Oh, Corban, that's the first milk I've tasted all this month!"

"How–how did you get here?" Corban asked, still looking at her as if she might vanish any moment.

"I walked," she said.

"Over the mountain?" Corban asked in amazement.

"Yes," Jennet said, and Jared watched as she tossed her head till her brown hair spun around her face as it had when she was a little girl. "Up the mountain and down the mountain and through the woods and over the roads, and whether I've still shoes on my feet is no matter, for I've new ones in my bundle–oh, where is my bundle?" She looked around her, alarmed at the thought of its loss.

Jared hurried outdoors and picked it up from the grass. He placed it on the table beside her, and she smiled gratefully up at him.

Corban reached out toward it. "What's in it?"

"My wedding dress," she said.

"Your wedding dress!" Corban gasped.

"Why yes; you said you'd come for me before June was out. Mother thought you hadn't because you'd heard about our village, and she bade me come to you."

"Heard what about your village?"

"That we've had sickness there."

"What sickness?"

"The spotted fever, but Corban–"

He let out an oath and backed away from her as if he had touched fire. "Get out of my house, Jennet Thaxter, get out of my house. I'll have no sickness here."

"But Corban, I–"

He reached forward and seized the noggin from which she had drunk her milk and dashed it on the hearth where the dull thud of its splintering pieces echoed in the room.

Jennet looked questioningly at Jared.

"Best do as he says, Jennet."

She moved reluctantly from the chair and started toward the door. "Jared, I've no place to go," she began, "and I'm so tired. This is my house, isn't it? I thought–"

Jared picked up the bundle and put it under his arm, then placed his hand lightly on her shoulder as they went out the door. "I'll find a place for you to stay," he said to her.

In the dark outside the house he looked at her earnestly. "Don't anger him, Jennet; he's suffered hard this spring and things prick him easily. Wait here for me till I get the mare."

He went back to the house, where Corban had picked up a broom and was sweeping the floor wildly as if the very dust of Jennet's feet held contamination. Jared laid his hand on his arm.

"Ease yourself, Corban, and hearken to reason. The sickness was not near Jennet, and no girl who can walk for two days and a night has anything brooding in her. I'll take her to Eliza for a while, but give me a word of comfort for her. She'll want to know when you'll be marrying."

Corban looked up dully and shook his head. "Not till harvest; I've too many things to do until then."

"A woman can ease a man's way, Corban."

Corban shook his head. "Not till harvest, if we get harvest."

Jared fetched the Gray One and sat Jennet on her back; then he walked beside her down the road.

"She's the filly that used to run in the pasture near your house," Jared said. "Would you know her now?"

"Of course I would." Jennet put out her hand and stroked the curving neck. "But she's grown fine and strong."

He smiled up at her. She moved her hand quickly from the Gray One's arched neck to Jared's thin shoulder. "Oh, Jared, I'm pained to tell you, but your father died last week."

"My father?" Jared repeated, stunned by the news. He had not thought anything could bend Eben Austin to its will, and it was hard to grasp the fact that death could. "Was it an accident?" he asked.

"No, Jared, it was spotted fever. My mother would not let me go near your house because of my being married so soon."

"Who buried him?"

"Nancy Austin did. No one else dared go near."

"Is she all right–and the girls?"

Jennet nodded. "Yes, and your little brother too. Had you forgotten him? He's near seven now and a fine hand for work."

"Jennet, are you sure that you were nowhere near the sickness?"

"I promise you that I was not, Jared. Do you think my mother would have let me come here if I could have brought it with me?"

They were nearing the Dunklees' now, and Jared went in first while Jennet stayed out in the soft June night.

The children were in bed and asleep, but John and Eliza were sitting by the trestle table. Eliza was sewing and John had the big Bible open before him. He was reading aloud from it in a deep voice. His face was lined with care, and Eliza's body was so thin that it gave Jared a quick pain in the heart to see it. Jared came forward quietly and sat down at the table beside them.

"The field is wasted, the land mourneth; . . . even all the trees of the field, are withered: because joy is withered away from the sons of men," John read.

"The seed is rotten under their clods, the garners are laid desolate, the barns are broken down; for the corn is withered.

How do the beasts groan! the herds of cattle are perplexed, because they have no pasture; yea, the flocks of sheep are made desolate. O Lord, to thee will I cry."

He turned the page.*"Yea, the Lord will answer and say unto his people, Behold, I will send you corn, and wine, and oil, and ye shall be satisfied therewith. . . . And ye shall eat in plenty, and be satisfied, and praise the name of the Lord your God, that hath dealt wondrously with you."*

John Dunklee closed the book quietly. "My mind's turned more to God these days. There is no other help."

"There never has been any other, good times or bad, if we but knew it," Jared added.

"Amen," Eliza murmured.

Jared soon told them of Jennet and her coming.

"Of course she can stay with us until the marrying," Eliza said quickly.

John nodded. "I don't know what we'll give her to eat, but she can stay with us."

"She'll work hard for you with the strength of her body and her two hands," Jared promised eagerly.

A thin, wiry line that in better days might have been called a smile spread across John's face. "All the hands in the world working for you won't do that much good if the weather doesn't work with you."

Jared went out and brought Jennet in and the Dunklees greeted her with the same kindness they had showed Jared when he first came to their door.

"But girl, you must be that spent," Eliza exclaimed, as she stirred among her shelves for something to give Jennet to eat.

"I slept well last night," Jennet said, "and I'm not really tired except in my feet, and they'll soon be rested."

"Did you sleep at a farmhouse on your way?" John Dunklee asked.

"No, in the woods."

"The woods!" he said. "But girl, there's bear in these parts, wolves too; more than one farmer has lost stock to them this spring, for there's little enough in the woods to feed on and they're prowling the farms."

Jennet tossed her head. "I found a hollow log and stopped up one end; then near the other I built a fire. The log was a safe place and no hungry creature was going to go through fire for a meal."

John nodded his head admiringly, and Jared laughed aloud at the wit of Jennet.

"That was a right sensible thing to do," Eliza Dunklee said as she put a plate of warm porridge before Jennet.

"Sensible!" Jared echoed to himself. His years in the world would have caused him to fix a bolder word to Jennet's deed. He would have called it bravery of the first order. But here in the country where every day called out the courage of the spirit, and bravery was a common thing, there was just one word for it–"sensible."

Later, riding up the hill in the dark, Jared knew that he must go immediately to his home on the other side of the mountains, that he must see his friends and family once again before it might be too late. During this first week of growing, the grain in the clearing would need no weeding. This week was the one week of the whole summer when he might be spared from tending it.

Early the next morning he packed his stencil kit and stowed brushes and paints in his saddlebags. Corban watched in amazement.

"So," he asked finally, "New England is too hard for you and you're going West?"

Jared looked up quickly. "Nothing of the kind, Corban Cristy. I'm just going itinerating for a week to help people take their minds off their troubles."

"You won't find anyone with cash to pay you."

"I'll do walls for nothing, just to get my brushes quickened again. But I'll be back in a week to tend my corn!"

"Your corn!" Corban laughed. "If you harvest enough to put in my hat I'll say 'well done.' Go along then, and good luck go with you."

Jared trotted briskly down the road, waving to the Dunklees at work in their fields, and Jennet with them; through the village he went, and then more slowly up the long road to the pass in the mountains. By noon he was on the high land and was riding over the same road he and Mr. Toppan had traveled more than six years ago.

Now he could gaze down into his valley. It looked wider, for there were more clearings than when he had lived in it; but the fields, instead of waving in all the lushness of June growth, were pinched and bare. There was green pasture-land, but the cattle grazing it were few, and the whole countryside had a deserted look, as if people were keeping to their homes.

It was dusk when he drew up to the Thaxters' door, and through the window he could see the family just seating themselves at the table. He bowed his head as grace was said and thanks offered for the meager supper. As they took up their spoons, Jared raised his hand and knocked on the wide oak slab that was the door.

"Who's there?" Father Thaxter called gruffly.

"A journeyman painter seeking shelter for the night and any job of work."

There was the sound of benches scraping the floor, then Father Thaxter opened the door; but it was Mother Thaxter, halfway across the room and still sitting at the table, who first recognized Jared. The years had lain lightly on her, and her feet were still swift in their errands of mercy. She sped across the room and folded Jared in her arms, holding him close to the ample bosom that had given comfort and haven to so many.

"Jared Austin," she cried, clasping his thin body tightly to her, "I knew you'd be back!" She held him off at arm's length, looking at him with hungry eyes. "Inches you've grown," she said finally, "but if you've put on a pound of flesh I don't see it!"

The Thaxter boys and Jennet's little sister were clamoring for recognition. Father Thaxter was wringing Jared's hand and trying to lead him to the table where a place was quickly laid for him. Thomas, the oldest boy, ran out to take the Gray One to the barn, first setting the saddle with its laden packs just inside the door.

Candles were lit and burned far down while they sat at table asking Jared question after question–first about Jennet's journey; then, assured of her safety and well-being, they asked Jared about himself, about the years since they had seen him, the work he had done, and the places he had been.

"We've heard you've got the master's touch in your work, Jared," Father Thaxter said proudly.

Jared inclined his head toward the saddle leaning near the door. "Tomorrow I shall do your north room, as I promised long ago." he said, "Then you shall see for yourselves."

Mother Thaxter sent the boys to the loft and tucked the little girl in the trundle bed, loath as they all were, though heavy with sleep, to leave the magic of the newcomer's company. Thomas stayed with his father around the table. Soon talk turned to the strange weather which had defied all attempts at growing.

"There'll be no corn and little enough hay, as far as I can see," Father Thaxter went on. "I've plowed up my fields for the third time in a month and am now putting them into turnips. Do what the weather likes, it can't do much to spoil turnips; they'll hold the cattle through the winter, and we can eat them too."

"It's hard times through all the valley then?" Jared asked, hoping to hear of some area that had been spared.

"Worse than hard and in some places worse than others," Father Thaxter said stoically. "We've had sickness here." Then his voice took on a new firmness. "But we've had an easier time in this land than our fathers and grandfathers, and if we can't make the best of a spell of bad weather we're not fit to work the land they opened for us."

It was not until an hour later, when Jared and Mother Thaxter were sitting alone by the banked coals of the fire that he heard what had happened to his father–how the fever that had been appearing here and there had laid him low and how no one dared go to his help for fear the fever would spread farther.

"Nancy's been alone in that house for a month, nursing them all. The boy had it when Eben was down but he has recovered. Now the girls are poorly."

"Thankful and Mary?" Jared asked, his words edged with horror and disappointment, for he had looked forward so much to seeing them.

Mother Thaxter nodded. "Yes, Nancy ties a handkerchief to the tree on the hill when she comes out at night and I bring what she wants to the hilltop in the morning, for none of us dare go near the house when we have young ones and menfolk of our own to care for. She hangs a red kerchief when she needs food and a white one for medicines." Mother Thaxter hesitated for a moment; then she went on, "Last week Nancy hung a black scarf from the tree–that was when your father died."

Jared's heart was heavy at the tale, but he had work to do and would press forward with it, leaving the contemplation of sorrow to other times.

"Mother Thaxter," he turned to her, "I've a field of my own I must tend and can stay away from it only a week, but I'll do your north room for you."

She smiled and laid her hand on his in a gesture of gratitude.

"Tonight I'll cut my stencils, if you'll spare me the candle," Jared went on, "and tomorrow I'll begin the work. The north room is small and when I'm minded I can work fast."

Suddenly her smile turned inside out, her eyes filled with tears, and her shoulders shook silently. Now it was Jared's turn to put his arms around her and try to bring comfort. He had never seen her weep before, and the strangeness of it stirred him.

"What is it, Mother Thaxter? I'd give you comfort if I knew what was needed."

She shook her head and was silent; then over long moments her shoulders eased their heaving. She dried her eyes and looked up at him.

"My heart's a sorry place with thinking of Jennet. Always I hoped she'd wait for you, but now she's pledged herself to Mr. Cristy."

Jared smiled. "And there's no finer man in New Hampshire! Oh, Mother Thaxter, I wasn't brave enough for Jennet. She has one her equal in Corban Cristy."

Mother Thaxter sighed. "She's brave and strong and I'm proud of her, but you've always been brave in spirit, Jared Austin, and that was the match for Jennet, not just another strong body like Mr. Cristy's."

Jared rose and went over to his saddlebag and started removing his kit. When he came back to the hearth with his knife and stencil papers, he turned to Mother Thaxter and with a smile such as she had never before seen on his face, spoke tenderly. "Jennet always said she wanted a man who had a hundred acres in his own name and farmed them all himself."

Mother Thaxter rose from the settle. "A hundred acres of the best land won't do anyone much good this year, but strength of spirit will," she said. She turned to leave the room, and Jared moved the candle nearer his work.

Chapter Nine

Jared worked steadily for two days. First he washed the walls all over with a pink that looked as if crushed raspberries had been used in the making–so soft and lovely a color it was; then he laced the edges of the room–the line near the ceiling, the line above the chair back and the line around the doors–with a looping green vine. It was a sturdy, healthy vine that looked capable of sending out more and more branches. On the open spaces of the walls he set flowers and a sunburst. So he brought to the north room all he had remembered through the years of the home that had been his first–the cheer of it and the grace of it, with the tendrils that bound his heart to it.

On the evening of the second day he surveyed with pride the simple design that enlivened the walls. During the past months he had turned carpenter and farmer, but his hands had lost none of their skill. It was proof of yet another of Mr. Toppan's oft-made sayings, "The more you do the richer you become, and the finer your work will be, for that much more goes into it."

"Yes, Mr. Toppan," Jared had said, as he had after all such remarks which were his due as an apprentice. Odd that he recalled them now and recognized their truth.

The Thaxters had few words with which to voice their pleasure when they stood in the room and let its gracious beauty enfold them. Mother Thaxter, looking at the walls, thought of the time when she had held Jared to life by telling him he was needed in the world. She had not known then that his hands would touch common things to loveliness, making them bear bud, blossom, and fruit. Everywhere, during this dark year of cold and famine, the cry was the same, "short crops, sickness, hard times"; yet here was Jared Austin bringing comfort to the countryside through beauty, warming a household, feeding its hungry hearts.

"There's food and fire there, Jared," Mother Thaxter said quietly, "but how 'tis done, I know not."

Father Thaxter nodded his head slowly. "It does me good to see such work," he said. "It'll do me even better when winter imprisons us."

"You used to feel the cold so when you were a little one." Mother Thaxter looked long at Jared, adding, "and something that wasn't cold used to make you shiver, but now–"

"Now I'm warmed through and through," Jared said with a smile. Then he leaned over and started to pack up his kit, wondering where it next would be unfolded.

That night Nancy Austin hung the black scarf on the tree. The morning wind billowed it and Jared, saddling the Gray One for an early start, saw it first.

"Mother Thaxter," he cried, hurrying into the house, "there's a black scarf on the tree."

She dropped the spoon with which she was stirring the porridge and turned to Jared. Her face paled quickly. "That's death, Jared. There's nothing any of us can do now."

"I must go to her."

"No, Jared," she said firmly, "you might take the fever yourself; you might take it to others." She laid her hand on his arm as if to restrain him.

"I must go. I'm not afraid for myself; and I promise you, Mother Thaxter, that I'll keep away from others till there is no danger."

Jared could be as firm as granite when his mind was settled on a thing and Mother Thaxter knew there was no withholding him. She put her arms around him then, as if he were still a reedy little boy.

"Jared, my dear one," she breathed softly, "when you were just a youngster, you gave your heart to God. 'Tis His love guiding you now, and I know He'll guide you aright."

Jared nodded. "That He will, indeed."

She kissed him warmly, then gave him breakfast.

There was a tender farewell with Mother Thaxter and a lively one with the rest of the family. Jared promised to come back with news of Jennet before the winter set in. Then he mounted the Gray One and turned her head up the hill to his father's house.

Nancy Austin opened the door that had known no knocking hand for a month. At the sight of a stranger on the stone, she passed her hand in bewilderment across her eyes, wondering if she was seeing things, so heavy had been the loneliness of the past weeks.

"No–no, you must not come here. Don't you see the mark I made on the door? There's sickness within," she said, closing the door, for dearly as she would have loved to talk with a peddler she knew she must not.

Jared made no move except to slide one booted foot against the door to keep it from closing.

"Nancy Austin, don't you know me?" he asked. "I've come to help you."

She leaned against the door, confused and puzzled. Her face was haggard and worn, her body thin. Somewhere behind her stood a pale boy with heavy black hair and dark eyes. She brushed her hand across her face again as if she were brushing time away; then a smile twisted her lips.

"It's Jared," she said hoarsely, "little Jared." Her hand went limp on the door and she backed away from it into the room.

Jared entered. The house was heavy with the oppressive sense of sickness.

"Is it Mary or Thankful?" he asked quietly.

"Oh, Jared, it's both of them. I did all I could, but it was like fighting a forest fire. I couldn't stop it." She reached forward and clutched his hand. "God must have sent you, for no one around here dares enter this house." She led him across the room and opened the door of the small bedroom.

Jared stepped across the threshold and caught his breath with a sob. He had longed to see Thankful and Mary in life, eager and joyous as he had remembered them. Now he saw them in death, white and stiff and still, marked by their illness. But though the years had brought them to maidenhood, death had returned them to childhood, so small they seemed, so innocent.

Nancy was leaning against the doorpost, sobbing and sobbing. Jared turned quickly to her. He knew the relief of tears and let her weep, but with his arms about her. During all the time Nancy Austin had been fighting for their lives, she had not once dared let sorrow have its way with her; now, with comfort at hand, she could loose the floodgates of her will.

"I tried–last night–" she said between sobs, "to bury them–but I couldn't."

Jared led her to a chair and made her comfortable. He talked quietly with her until anguish eased itself into sorrow, and sorrow began groping dimly along a way of peace; then he left her. He found his way to his father's workshop and there began measuring boards for a coffin. The pale, wide-eyed boy followed him.

"Young Eben," Jared said, taking the small rough hand between his, "can you find me a piece of soapstone in the old quarry near the woods?" He described its size with gestures and added, "A little higher than it is wide."

The boy nodded.

"Then fetch it here and I'll show you how we can cut through sorrow."

Jared soon made the simple pine box that was large enough for two bodies that were wasted and thin; then he turned to the stone Eben had found for him. Working carefully with a sharp-pointed tool, he inscribed letters on the stone. When he had finished, he drew the wondering boy to him.

"Have you learned to read yet?" Jared asked.

The boy inclined his head. "Thankful taught me last winter."

"Then read these words."

The boy bent forward and read slowly.

"THANKFUL AND MARY AUSTIN
How friendly seems the vast unknown
Since they have entered there."

Eben looked up quickly at Jared. A gleam, like the light from a small candle, was in his face, "Is that true, Jared?"

Jared nodded. "Even as little girls, they loved God with all their hearts–I remember it well. They've just gone ahead of us to Heaven, to be there to greet us." He laid a gentle hand on the boy's shoulder. "Now, let me see if you can wield a spade as a farmer should."

They crossed the field together, and Eben pointed out the curved mound near an apple tree where Nancy had laid the boy's father. They struck their spades to the earth and dug, and though the frost had firmed the topsoil, they were soon below it and in the soft earth. Young Eben worked well, with strength of body and a knowing hand, more than once glancing up at Jared for a word of praise which sent him back to the task with new vigor.

At sundown the half brothers and Nancy Austin carried the pine box to the deep trench. They laid it in gently, as though careful not to stir the slumber of the little girls; then Jared and Eben shoveled the earth back and made the mound smooth. The stone was fixed in its place at the head of the mound. Jared knelt first; then Nancy dropped to her knees beside him, and the boy beside her. Jared looked to Nancy for the prayer, but her face was sad and heavy. Her eyes were dry and her lips set as if to enforce bravery, and Jared knew that just then her heart was no soil from which prayer might grow; so he lifted his head and prayed aloud, committing Thankful and Mary to their heavenly Father.

"Amen," Nancy said as his words faded into the twilight.

Later that evening, after supper, and after the boy had been tucked into the trundle bed, Jared sat long with Nancy Austin by the hearth. He talked with her about the farm and the crops, giving her advice here and comfort there, so neatly interwoven that Nancy thought it was her own mind speaking and felt stronger for the strength in herself.

"Sometimes the frost heaves out our walls and we have to build them again, and sometimes we have to build our lives up again," Jared said, "but there are plenty of stones in the fields and there is plenty of vigor in the spirit of man. You and young Eben have fine land to work with, Nancy Austin."

She smiled. "And we've got spirit too; we'll keep the farm going and make it thrive."

Jared rose to go.

"Jared," she said with a boldness that surprised him, "when I sell the apple crop this September, can I hire you to do my walls for me?"

"You can, but I'll not take your money. I'll do your walls with the best that's in me."

"And I'll pay you for what I get–it will be the apples that will do it."

"All right then, Nancy Austin, I'll be back before all the leaves have fallen."

He was soon riding off into the night.

An easy journey it would have been, to reach Cristy's by morning, especially since the Gray One was so fresh; but Jared rode slowly and stopped along the way to rest for the night. Then, when morning came, he left the road and followed a brook into the woods. Finding a place where it widened into a pool with a sandy bottom, he tethered the

Gray One nearby and took off all his clothes; then plunged into the water and scrubbed himself with the sand.

Garment by garment, all but his boots, he took his clothing into the pool with him. Washing each piece vigorously, then rinsing where the water ran fresh over the stones, he hung his clothes on the trees to dry. Sitting quietly on a stone, he let the summer wind and the high sun dry his body. He knew that properly he should have burned the clothes he had worn into a house where spotted fever was, but he had nothing else with him to wear and little else at Corban Cristy's; so he turned to the cleansing action of water and waited for the sun to do its work.

It was evening when he got back. Quietly he took the Gray One's saddle and bridle into the barn and turned her loose in the pasture, and as quietly he went into the house and left a note for Corban telling him not to look for him for a while longer. Then with a hoe, and some bread and cheese done up in a handkerchief, he sought the high clearing. There would be shelter among the trees, water at a spring he knew, berries and roots to augment his small store of food, and he would keep his promise to Mother Thaxter–not to go near anyone for a while after being in a house where the fever had been.

He slept on the edge of the clearing and, waking at the first streak of dawn, saw the seed he had planted a week ago like a fine green carpet before him. He hoed it then, small as it was, and he hoed it every day during the growing weather of that strange summer. The heat of the sun got into the cool earth, and though the nights were cold–still frosty in the low places–the corn in the clearing grew tall and green.

The frosts in the early and latter part of June had taken many a man's third and fourth plantings. Now, though the weather had at last swung into a stride of warmth, there had been no rain for weeks and no dew either. The few crops that had escaped the frosts looked pitifully meager as they struggled on out of the dry, dusty earth. The grass in meadow and pasture was still light and backward, and when haying days should have been well underway, few farmers saw any sense in cutting.

So widespread were the weather conditions that the weekly papers had begun to find them a chief topic of news–sometimes in an endeavor to explain them, sometimes to make light of them, sometimes to give advice for the planting of alternative crops. As the season advanced, the harvest was a gloomy prospect despite the rains that came at last, but the Yankee farmer could be trusted to be ingenious.

The hard times found people responding to them in different ways. There were some farmers whose work with the land made them philosophical and unemotional. They stuck with the soil in the same determined way their fathers had, braving the terrors of the wilderness and the depredations of the Indians because desire was strong within them to be masters in a free land. There were those who–brave enough when things went right–found the strain of hard times and the prospect of harder ones not to their liking. Those were the men who became fretful and restive, hearkening to tales that itinerants told of broad lands in the opening West, lands of rich earth where the sun warmed it well and winter ceased as it should in March.

There was yet another group of men, a small but dangerous group, who had lost heavily but who could still spend their time in idle gossip. Ignorant and cowardly, they became easily alarmed at any phenomenon and sank into superstition. All the strength they should have been using with sickle or flail, had the weather allowed, went to their tongues as they talked about the cruel times and tried to find a reason for them.

"We were all right until that painter fellow came our way," Ephraim Twiss muttered to such a group assembled one day at Dan True's.

"No one has seen him for a long while now," Dan put in, seeking to keep the peace.

"I saw him yesterday," a bearded man said, wiping his lips as he put down his mug. "He was coming out of Cristy's woods, and as sure as I'm standing here he was talking with the Devil–writing his name in his book!"

"Oh, come now," put in Dan True.

"Yes," the bearded man went on, "and the Devil was that pleased with his bargain that he jumped right up in the air and disappeared."

"Just let there be one more freeze in this spell of growing weather," Twiss said darkly, "and we'll know where to lay the blame."

Corban Cristy came often to the inn these days, but not to hearken to the talk of the discontents. He was too full of a need for action to worry about mere talk, but his ears were quick to catch news of the West. The frosts that had taken his plantings had left him with little to do, and a restlessness was coursing with the red blood in his veins. If it was true that the West was such a land, he told himself, if he could be sure that it was true, he would sell his place for whatever anyone would give him and ride Young Meteor out to the Western Reserve.

"That's a long way for a horse to go who's had thin pasture this summer," Dan True said restrainingly.

Corban shook his head. "I've gone hungry myself but Young Meteor hasn't. He's as fit as he ever was, for he's had the hay and grain the others haven't." Then he laughed. "Always keep a means of flight is what the highwayman said–and it's a good saying."

True winked one eye at Corban. "That lass of yours– she'd like the West too, I expect?"

Corban was silent for a moment. "It's an odd thing, Dan, but I've got out of thinking of marrying, I've had so much else on my mind."

"She won't go long unwed," True reminded him.

"No other man is going to have her while I'm around," Corban said hotly.

He was soon riding home at a good speed, stopping off at the Dunklees' on the way. They were busy in the fields, haying the light crop that was no more than a cutting of grass. Eliza and the young children were working as hard as John, not letting so much as a wisp go off on the wind, and Jennet was gleaning after them.

Corban laughed aloud. " 'Tisn't worth the time you're putting on it, John Dunklee."

"Maybe not," Dunklee said, wiping his hot face, "but if it's all we're going to get, the stock will think it's worth it when January comes."

Corban waved to Jennet, who had come trudging up the dusty lane, a bundle of short hay in her arms. "Ho, lass! How would you like to come West with me?"

She quickened her steps until she stood beside him. "Corban," she panted, laying one hand on Young Meteor's heaving flank, "what are you saying?"

"I've a notion to go West."

"And leave your land?" The horror of such action was wide writ on her tired face.

"Leave this mad weather," he said.

She reached up and caught his hand. "But Corban, we've got to beat the weather–the way our fathers beat the wilderness."

Young Meteor plunged forward and Jennet stepped swiftly sidewards to avoid his heavy feet. Corban reined him in, then wheeled quickly and galloped down the lane. Taking a stone wall in his stride, he raced across his own fields. The dust swirled around him. Jennet put her hand to her eyes.

"Don't mind him now." Eliza came up behind her. "Hard times strike all men differently; some turn to drink and some turn restless."

Jennet bent over to pick up the hay she had lost from her bundle.

"Wait till you see the mess of blackberries Reuben and Delight have brought from the woods," Eliza said comfortingly; "at least they are growing still. "

Jennet looked up, and smiled into Eliza's face. "I'm hungry, Eliza." The tone was that of a little girl waiting over-long for her supper.

Eliza laughed. "We'll know those words well before the winter's out, but at least none of us will have to say we're starving."

Corban found Jared at the house and greeted him with pleasure, for weeks had passed since their last meeting.

"I knew you were near when I saw the Gray One in pasture," Corban said, "but I figured you had your own work to attend to so I made no bother of finding you."

"I've been tending my corn."

"How is it coming on?"

Jared smiled proudly. "The rain and these warm days have given it a great leap," he said eagerly. "We'll harvest a goodly number of bushels, Corban, at this rate."

"We?" Corban laughed not unkindly. "You keep your mite, Jared; I've a mind to go West where the land is wider. These fiddling fields and fickle weather don't suit my fancy."

"But you've cleared your land," Jared exclaimed, "and built your house and found your wife. You can't go away now!"

There was nothing like crossing Corban to make him set as a flint. "Can't I? We'll see," he said bitterly. "I'll take the lass along with me, and we'll build again in a land where a man can call his soul his own."

"Jennet's New Hampshire born and bred. Do you think she'll leave the hills for the plains that easily?"

"She will if I say so," Corban answered quickly.

The next morning it was as if Corban had forgotten their talk of the West, for the day was hot and the crops were reaching forward. He worked hard in his fields, hoeing his potatoes; and with Jared's help and persuasion he even started haying a small meadow. The air had a refreshing stillness to it, for the warm sun and recent rains had given such an upsurgence to the grass that the cattle were feeding greedily and the lowing that had marked their hunger since spring had ceased.

After they had finished their work together, Jared went up through the woods to the clearing. No one but Corban knew of this venture of his, and he only laughed at it. Someday, Jared thought, he would bring Jennet up and show her the green stalks waving so boldly–the only cornstalks in the countryside. Then he decided that perhaps he'd keep it a secret until the grain had come. Twilight came over the land, and Jared caressed the corn as he walked through it. Hoeing it so frequently had hastened its maturity, and silky tassels were beginning to show. He would hoe no more now until the ears had formed.

Week after week of growing weather had gone by and August was nearly over. The hard work of the farmers and the luxuriant flourishing of the past few weeks had given a different face to the countryside. Men were freer with each other, sharing less of foreboding and more of hope. The strange tales about Jared that had been circulating through superstitious minds had all but ceased.

Dan True, riding past Corban Cristy's one day, hailed Jared at work in the field with Corban. Riding up to them, True began to make plans with Jared for decorating his walls after harvest.

"I'll be glad to take the brush again, Dan True," Jared said with a smile, "and glad to do your walls."

"If he does the like of mine, you'll have half the country coming to you just to see them," Corban put in, for he had an honest pride in Jared's work, and a loyalty to him.

"After the harvest then," True said as he swung his horse around. "I'll pay you well and give you all we can in the way of food and shelter while you're at work on the walls."

But one might as well have said "after Doomsday" as "after harvest," for the uncertainty of it. There was to be little harvest during that year of 1816–at least, little of the harvest men had become accustomed to gathering. Harvest of other kinds might be garnered, but they would not be the sort men talked about.

The last day of August had been hot and humid, like many other days that month. No farmer, working in his fields in a desperate effort to spur the earth to further production, had any indication that it would be the last day of such work. The storm that roared over the land that night was unexpected and utterly devastating. Wind lashed hail along its path; rain edged with snow beat against house and barn.

Jared listened to the storm that night as it hurled itself against the house. Lying there silently in the dark, he might well have shivered in the uncontrollable way he had shivered when he was a child–but he did not. He might well have feared what Corban Cristy would do; but fear had left his heart on an April night, months ago, and faith had come in its place. There was no need to lie there and wonder what would happen. When morning came, it would show them what they each must do.

It was a ghastly sight that greeted New England farmers the next morning. Again the land lay blighted by frost–and for the last time; there would be no more growing weather this year before the winter set in. The turnips and apples were unharmed; the potatoes, though small, could be dug and stored away. Here and there a handful of crops that had been spared by the vagaries of wind and frost could be harvested, but the corn had been cut off, and corn was the standby for the farmer. Some farmers were well enough off to command money to buy grain from other states for their stock and foodstuffs for their families; but less fortunate ones faced a grim winter.

Corban had stopped his ears that night at the noise of the storm, but the dull light of morning compelled him to look out over his fields. He did so in silence; then he turned to Jared, and his words came from between set teeth. "I'm through–" With a string of oaths, he stamped out to the barn. When he returned he said briefly, "You fetch the lass. Tell her we're going West today."

"Corban, think again," Jared begged.

Corban's face was terrible in its intensity. "Tell her what I have said–and bring her here."

Jared knew there was nothing to say to Corban when his mind was set. He left him, hoping that time would ease the man and his mind would change. Saddling the Gray One, he rode down the road through the white death of the morning to the Dunklees'.

Knocking lightly on the door, he entered the kitchen and found the family seated at the table. On it was a trencher of blackberries, and before each person, a plate of thin porridge. The children looked up and smiled at Jared. Eliza moved over and made a place for him without looking up. Jared saw the lines tears had made down her cheeks and knew she was too proud to have him see that her spirit had been broken. Jennet glanced up at Jared. Her eyes were wide and dark shadowed; looming in them was the bewilderment a child feels when all sources have failed to answer its questioning.

John Dunklee put his head in his hands and said hoarsely, "Give us the grace, Jared; I can't this morning."

Jared laid one hand on Eliza's thin shoulder, the other on Delight's; then he raised his eyes.

"Father, we thank Thee this morning for turnips and apples and wild berries–for pheasants and partridge and deer–for cold spring water and the warmth of fire on a hearth. Above all, we thank Thee for the love Thou hast shown to each one of us. Make us strong in spirit and help us to trust Thee during these hard times."

"Amen," the children answered.

"Amen," Jennet responded, the sound like a sob.

They picked up their spoons and began to eat.

"I've not come to share your meal," Jared said, "but with a message from Corban for Jennet."

He glanced at her. "Corban wants you, Jennet; he's going West today. He wants that you should be ready to go with him in as short a time as possible."

Jennet went white. "No!" she cried aloud. "I won't go!" And terror was in her face.

John Dunklee looked at her. "Jennet, that's no way to speak of your husband's plans."

"He's not my husband–not yet." She shook her head and her hair tossed on her shoulders.

"But you're promised," John reminded her.

Jennet looked wildly around the table, seeking someone to help her.

Eliza laid her hand on the girl's arm, then she turned to Jared. "She doesn't love him enough–yet–to go that far with him. Restrain him for a few days, Jared."

"Restrain the tide," Jared said. "You know what he is when his mind is set."

Eliza looked at Jennet. "Come, girl, eat what's on your plate and go up the hill with Jared. Have a few words of your own with Corban, and try to understand him. Let them be easy words, Jennet, my dear," Eliza went on, "for it's a terrible thing when your man loses the fruit of the earth, and it's your place to comfort him."

Jared and Jennet walked slowly up the hill, leading the Gray One between them. Words were not there for them; so they walked in silence.

Corban was waiting on the doorstone. Young Meteor was saddled and stood near. Jennet walked toward Corban slowly, while Jared took the Gray One to the barn. Jared debated leaving them and going up the hill to the clearing, then thought better of it and stayed at hand. When the even tone of voices in conversation changed to the sharp pleading of a woman and the thunderous commanding of a man, Jared came around to the front of the house.

"I won't go," Jennet was saying, stamping her foot and tossing her head, "not this day nor any other day. I'll stay here and keep your house and look after your creatures until you find your senses and come back."

"Look after the creatures with a barn as empty as a blown seed pod?" Corban roared.

"But what will become of them–the cows, the sheep–if you leave them?"

"Let them stray. Let them go back to wildness again. They are naught but skin and bone now, and there isn't a cow that's giving milk."

Jennet's voice dropped sternly. "You can't abandon the creatures any more than you can your land."

"Oh, can't I?" he said bitterly. "You're just afeard to go with me," he muttered with a snarl in his voice.

Then Jennet blazed. "Afeard, Corban Cristy! I've never known that word and I never will. It's you who are afeard to stay and see the winter through!"

"Corban–Jennet–" Jared stepped between them. "There's suffering enough in the world today. Must you speed it on the wind as well?"

"She's bound to stay, and I'm bound she'll go," Corban said darkly.

"I'm bound I'll stay and care for his stock and his land until he comes back again."

"It's madness," Corban said. "The land is dead and the stock is dying."

"It's kindness," she corrected him, and her eyes, no longer blazing, were like deep waters mirroring his might. She reached forward and took his hand in hers. "I'll be waiting here for you, Corban Cristy, and I'll hold naught against you."

"If I go," he said impatiently, "and I am going, I'll not come back for you or anyone."

"But this house that you have made, Corban–" she began.

"Let it stand," he said. "Let it rot." Pushing her away with the hand she had been clasping, he turned and went toward Young Meteor.

"Corban," Jared said, "you can curse the land and whip the hide off a beast, but it's a terrible thing to break a woman's heart." He looked straight into the man's hard, white face, and for a moment there was no sound between them but the sobbing of the girl huddled on the doorstone.

"My mind is set," Corban Cristy said. "Good-bye, Jared Austin. You're the only man in the world I've not lost my temper with, and I don't want to now." His foot was in the stirrup; his heavy leg was flung over the saddle.

"Corban—" Jared began, reaching for words to stay him.

Corban put his hand into his pocket and drew out two crumpled papers which he pressed into Jared's hands.

"I thought the lass might act like this—good riddance to her." He swore a long oath. "What man wants a wife with a will like that?" Digging his heels into Young Meteor's ribs, Corban swung the rearing stallion around angrily.

Now there was no sound on the morning air but the hard clapping of iron-shod hooves on iron-fast ground.

Jared watched Corban racing down the road.

"If he could not go like that, he would go mad," Jared murmured.

Leaving Jennet to a sorrow she must face alone, Jared turned and went into the house. How strange the stenciled walls seemed now—all the little bells waiting to ring in happiness and looking as if they might have to wait forever.

Jared sat down at the table he and Corban had made together and opened the crumpled papers. On one of them, written in Corban's clumsy handwriting, Jared saw the words:

TO WHOM IT MAY CONCERN
The lands that I have cleared and the stock that I have raised, I leave to Jared Austin. God knows what he, a painter, will do with them, but so be it.

Corban Cristy

With fingers far from steady, Jared opened the other paper and read:

TO WHOM IT MAY CONCERN
This house that I have made and had decorated I leave to Jennet Thaxter to do with as she thinks best until the day of her death.
                                                      Corban Cristy

Jared folded the papers in his hands and sighed. "God help the man with more strength of muscle than of spirit," he said.

He rose from the table and went to the barn to see how the stock were faring–his creatures now, his acres; and he, whose sole possessions had been a stenciler's kit and a willing mare, wondered what he would do in this starvation year with such doubtful wealth.

Chapter Ten

The sun was shining bravely and the warmth of midday rested on the blighted land when Jared came around the corner of the house to Jennet. She was sitting on the door-stone, holding her head high. Her eyes were dry, and except for a paleness to her face there was no sign of her sorrow; but there was something about her which made her like one who has looked deeply into life. Jared sat down on the grass in front of her.

"Jennet," he said quietly, "Corban left a note for you. It says the house is yours."

Her eyes widened in surprise.

"No one can dispute it," Jared went on, "for it's signed like a deed in its own right."

Jennet was silent for a long time; then she spoke slowly. "That was kind of him." Her voice was as soft as the flowing of water over stones. She looked up at Jared earnestly. "But Corban has stock–what is to be done with them? How can I feed them through this winter?"

Jared shook his head sadly. "They'll have to be sold, Jennet, all but one or two, and we'll have to work hard and fast to harvest feed enough for those two this winter."

"We'll work together," she said, smiling at him, "as we used to in the old days when we were brother and sister. But what shall we have for ourselves to eat?"

"I've a secret, Jennet." He leaned closer to her as if to keep his words from even the wind. "I've wanted to share it with you this long time." He told her of the corn he had planted in the clearing. "And it's got ears on it now, as golden as a king's ransom!"

She clapped her hands as he spoke; then her face looked troubled. "But last night–have you seen it since the storm?"

He shook his head. "I'm wanting to go there now."

She rose quickly from the doorstone and followed him to the barn, where they found scythes and baskets. If the storm had laid low the corn and the frost had withered it, the sooner it was cut the better. When they reached the clearing, Jennet shouted as she saw tall stalks flapping in the breeze, but their green was edged with brown.

"The frost has lain here too," Jared said, "but not the wind or the hail." He looked around at the forest enclosing them. "Oh, goodly trees, how well you have sheltered my corn!"

He moved in and out among the tall stalks, feeling the ears for their soundness and turning back the shucks here and there to see the kernels just full in the milk. He came back to stand beside Jennet, and Jennet thought that at that moment she had never seen such a light as was shining in his thin face.

"There's food here for many," Jared said almost reverently, "and what's even more than food–seed for next year's sowing. But we must lose no time in harvesting it, for the rot of the frost will soon start its work."

They took a basket and moved through the corn, plucking off the ears with their dried tassels and heavy weight of kernels, emptying the basket time after time until they had a great pile at one side of the field. When all the ears had been gathered in, Jared took the scythe and started cutting the stalks while Jennet followed him, picking them up and binding them into bundles.

Jared laughed aloud. "Here's food for the Gray One and the brindled cow and perhaps a pair of sheep."

"Oh!" Suddenly Jennet gave a small gasp. "Food! I'm so hungry, Jared. Is it wicked of me always to be so hungry?"

"Jennet, shall we leave the work and go back to the house?" He dropped his scythe and came to stand beside her.

She shook her head and smiled at him. "No, you stay on with the work. I'll go down to my house and fetch something back for us to eat."

"That's good," he said with a nod, "for if I can keep cutting we'll have the clearing done by nightfall; then–come wind, come weather!"

Fleet as a cloud before the wind, Jennet was off down the path through the woods. Jared watched her go, then bent to his task with a lightness at his heart that made him want to shout for joy as he saw the corn yield its tall weight to his scythe.

Corban Cristy had ridden through the village at such a pace that he had scarcely seen the group of men gathered outside True's inn. But they had seen him and they knew without a question who it was, for there was no horse so powerful in all that countryside as Young Meteor, and no rider so reckless as Corban Cristy.

"Whither bound?" Ephraim Twiss called to him.

Corban reined in Young Meteor long enough to shout, "West! I'm through with this land and–" but the stallion plunged at the sudden check to his speed and Corban's words were lost.

"He's riding as if the Devil himself were on his heels," one man said.

The crowd echoed his words until Ephraim Twiss swore that he saw the Devil trailing a ball of fire at Young Meteor's hooves.

"What did he look like?" someone cried out.

"Look like?" Twiss bellowed. "None other than that painter fellow with his skinny body."

So a roar went up from the crowd, a demand for retribution on the painter fellow. It was not the frosts alone and the blighted land that the men laid to his account; a dozen recriminations were piled against his name. Each man voiced his grievance and swore vengeance. It mattered nothing to them that the calamities of the year were widespread; in their community the brunt of the blame was fixed upon Jared Austin.

The men moved into the inn and Dan True watched them warily. Ephraim Twiss raised his mug and drained it. "Did you hear what Cristy said–that he was through with the land and the painter too?"

"Aye, we did," a husky voice answered.

"The house has been bedeviled, sure enough, and a man like Corban Cristy will stay in it no longer."

"Perhaps that painter's a witch," Twiss muttered, "and we know what should be done with witches!"

"Aye, that we do!"

The voices rose in wrath until Dan True sought to restrain them by speaking a word for Jared.

"So, he's bewitched you too!" Twiss screamed shrilly.

True leveled his eyes at Twiss, then swept the crowd with his scathing glance. "Not a drop or crust will any one of you have again under my roof until you stop this madness," he said. "You've all had too much as it is." Taking his keys from his pocket, he rattled them before their faces as if to show the men that he could keep his word.

"Come men, the day is getting on," Twiss shouted. "Shall we make the devil pay for his deeds, or not?"

"Make him pay!" they roared in answer.

"Burn him with all his fiendish wall writings!"

Taking up whatever implements they had or grabbing whatever was within their reach in the yard of the inn–shovels, axes, pitchforks–the men formed into a body behind Ephraim Twiss and started up the road that led to

Corban Cristy's house. Anger made them sullen, and the lust for vengeance gave a heavy rhythmic stride to their booted feet.

Eliza Dunklee saw them when, two hours later, they passed her place–a strange band of men with a strange assortment of implements, treading the dusty road with grim deliberateness. She wondered what harvest they were bound to gather and thought to call out to them, but a dread came into her heart at the unkempt, ragged appearance of the men. When she saw who their leader was and knew him for a man no honest farmer would trust, she called Tobit to her and bade him watch the babe in its cradle while she went to the fields behind the house to summon Reuben and Delight from their work.

Jennet Thaxter saw the strange body of men just as she came out of the woods and was running across the meadow to the house. She stopped for a moment, wondering where they were bound, for there was something about their black silence and the dull thud of their feet that spelled evil. Then horror knocked within her, stilling the gnawing of hunger at her ribs, as she saw the body of men turn into the road that led up to her house. She tried to shout to them but the breath was trapped within her; then the wit that was her fiber moved her feet. Deftly she veered from the path and darted across the short space of meadow into the barn and through it to the house, reaching the front door a moment or two before the men.

She pushed one hand through her hair to lighten its disorder and laid the other on her heart to still its wild beating. For one perilous moment, her eyes sped around the entryway with its stencils–the little bells waiting to ring, the pineapples offering hospitality; then she threw the door wide open and stepped boldly out across the threshold.

"Good-day, gentlemen," she said. "Mr. Cristy is not at home, but perhaps you'll tell your business to me."

Ephraim Twiss moved forward, and the men broke their rank and swarmed around the doorstone.

"It's not Corban Cristy we want, but the painter fellow that's been living here."

"Oh, he–" Jennet began.

Then the crowd began roaring "devil," "witch," and through their briny oaths Jennet caught the words "Burn the house down and him within it."

"Quiet, men," Twiss roared. He turned to Jennet. "This house is no place for a woman now. We have work to do here and you'd best be leaving, but before you go–tell us where the fellow is."

A man on the edge of the crowd raised his axe and swung it around his head, then hurled it through the air to sink deep into one of the doorposts. Another had gone into the house by the back way and had brought coals from the hearth to kindle outside.

"Stop!" Jennet cried in a voice so imperative that every man instinctively moved back a pace. "Put out that fire, Ephraim Twiss."

And Twiss, almost without knowing that he was obeying her, stamped on the coals and cuffed the man who had been kindling them.

"Let not one of you lay a finger on my house," Jennet said, tossing her head as if to challenge them to something they dared not do.

"Your house?" Twiss asked.

"My house," Jennet replied, "as much mine as if James Madison himself had given it to me. There's a deed in my own name, signed and secure."

Jennet ripped the axe out of the doorpost and flung it over the heads of the crowd, so low that a dozen men ducked and bit their lips in fear. The axe landed with a thud on the earth. The men backed away from the door–all but Ephraim Twiss, who stood adamant.

"We'll spare the house but not that devil with a painter's kit. Tell us his whereabouts and we'll leave."

"You must think I know much, to tell you the way an itinerant takes," she said.

"He was here this morning–I saw him," a man shouted from the crowd.

"He's hiding in the woods, I'll warrant. Come on, men, let's set fire to the woods and let the devil perish in his own element!"

Jennet laughed at them. "The fire will spread to your own woods." But the threat had little effect on the men who were already moving away from the house. "Men," she called, "he'll be back here in three days' time; can't you wait until then?"

They hesitated and murmured together.

"Yes," someone shouted out from the back of the crowd.

"Yes," they all shouted in chorus, for the satisfaction of burning woodland was as nothing to wreaking vengeance on the man himself.

"Ephraim Twiss." Jennet turned to him. "This is a free country, and if Jared Austin gives himself up to you, you must try him fairly in the Meeting House three days from now."

Ephraim nodded. Confused by a wit that ran ahead of his rage, he was compelled to admit that the girl was right. There was a heavy case against the painter fellow, but he had a right to a free trial.

"Summon your Justice of the Peace and have your witnesses at hand," Jennet said inexorably.

"Who would that be, men?" Twiss called to his crowd.

"Why, Randall Eveleth," the bearded man shouted back.

"Three days from today, then–in the Meeting House," Twiss muttered, "and it's a dozen men against the painter to one for him."

"Let him defend himself when the time comes," Jennet said shortly, "and let the decision be with Mr. Eveleth. Is that agreed?"

"Agreed," Twiss echoed.

Slowly, sulkily, Ephraim Twiss turned and started away, with his men following him. Jennet watched them go down the road until they were out of sight.

Jared, at work in the clearing, scything and bundling and standing the cornstalks, realized that darkness was almost upon him and Jennet had not yet returned. She'd had more than enough time to collect food and bring it back. Thinking that something had kept her from returning, he put his scythe over his shoulder and started down through the woods.

On the edge of the meadow he met Jennet. Her face was pale and her eyes were the eyes of one who had been kindling sparks, but her step was firm. She carried a basket over her arm.

"Jennet," he cried to her, "is all well?"

She came running to him. "Don't leave the woods, Jared," she said quickly, pushing him back into the shadow of the trees.

"Jennet, what–" he began.

"Hush," she said; "don't talk. Let us eat what I have in the basket and then go back for the corn."

She drew him down beside her at the base of a tree and started to divide the scant meal. They ate hungrily.

Suddenly Jennet asked, "How long will it take us to husk the corn and stow it in the granary?"

"Perhaps a week," he said, "if we work at it steadily."

"Could we do it in three days if we worked very hard?"

He nodded. "Perhaps, but there is no hurry now, Jennet. No harm can come to the corn and there's grain enough there for all the village to share, with seed for the spring sowing."

"Frost can't harm it now but the wrath of man can. Oh, Jared–" She looked up at him; then she told him of the men who had stormed the house. "They promised a trial in three days' time but Jared, my darling, there's a dozen of them to speak against you, and who's to speak for you? They'll drown out the Dunklees' words and when they're as crazed as they are, they'll imagine a thousand things against you. I've heard too many tales from years ago of houses burned and men and women destroyed by the madness of their own people. "

Jared looked at her. He had heard only two words of all her talk. He smiled at her, a smile that gave to his face the beauty he saw so readily in all things.

She stared at him. "Jared Austin, you'd think I'd brought you good news!"

"You have, Jennet."

She shook her head slowly.

He took her hand and pressed it to his lips. "You called me your darling."

Then Jennet smiled and flung her arms around him. "Oh, Jared, what a crazed lass I was to get promised to anyone but you!"

"I asked you when we were children if you would marry me," he reminded her. "You never said yes, and I never believed you meant no, but you did say you would marry a man who had a hundred acres in his own name."

Jennet bowed her head in shame, and Jared lifted it tenderly. "I'm that man now, for Corban's left the farm to me." Then he laughed. "But I'm no farmer!"

She looked hard at him. His face was a white blur in the night about them but she saw its light, a light that she knew would shine for her all the days of her life.

"You're the only man in all this countryside who has made corn grow this year!"

She sighed deeply. She was tired, and hunger still gnawed at her, but the comfort of his arms around her was strength and assurance and peace.

"Who will speak for you, Jared, at the trial?" she asked after a few moments.

"The corn will speak for me," he said quietly, "and it has a tongue that hungry men will understand."

They parted then, in the woods; Jennet to return to the Dunklees and Jared to seek the shelter he had made earlier in the summer at the clearing.

For the next three days they worked together from dawn till dusk, husking the corn. At night Jared loaded panniers on the Gray One's back and brought the corn down to the granary in the barn. It was hard work. Backs were bent nearly double in weariness, and fingers grew calloused from pulling the husks; but there was laughter and talk between them and plans for the future, and a kiss now and then over a bushel of golden corn, and hunger less querulous for the promise that lay in the flowing bins of the granary.

In the evenings, before Jennet went to the Dunklees for the night, she would leave something hot for Jared in the barn. It might be only milk thickened with flour or a bit of barley boiled in milk, but it tasted good to Jared. In the mornings, when she returned to the clearing, she brought news with her of the countryside.

"Ephraim Twiss got word to Randall Eveleth," she announced one morning, "and he's promised to be at the Meeting House at four tomorrow afternoon. Everyone is that excited, Jared. They're coming from miles around to the trial!"

"Men like a spectacle, no matter what it is," Jared said. "One day Mr. Toppan and I arrived in a city where there was to be a hanging the next morning. There was great excitement, and the crowd of spectators gathered to witness it grew with the hours; but the poor sinner hung himself in his cell, and the disappointment of the crowd was terrible to see."

"You could go away, Jared," she reminded him.

"But I won't," he told her. "I've never disappointed anyone and I don't intend to now."

"There's snow on the mountains, Jared, and winter will be on the minds of many in that courtroom."

He did not seem worried. "I'm not surprised, for the nights have been cold. The geese are migrating already; have you seen them? Early this morning I saw some on their way south."

"The leaves are falling quickly," she added wistfully.

"After we're married, Jennet, and before the snow lies deep, we'll go over the mountain to see your mother and father, and I have walls to do there for Nancy Austin."

"There'll be more and more people wanting you to do their walls," she said proudly, "but you'll have to keep some time for your land."

"I will," he said with a nod. Then he went on, "When Squire Tallant told me that a man had to be something of a farmer to survive, I didn't know what he meant, but now I do. Oh, Jennet!" His eyes flashed with happiness. "A fine thing it will be, to itinerate during the winter and work with the land the rest of the year!"

They went on with their husking in silence for a while.

"What news is there of the harvest elsewhere?" Jared asked her suddenly.

She shook her head. "Little enough but loss. Last night John came in with a tale of a farmer farther north who is harvesting some corn and has promised to sell it to the people for five silver dollars a peck!"

Jared let out an exclamation. "Who can pay that for long?"

"What will you ask for your corn, Jared?"

He shook his head. "Not one penny for a bushel, nor a name on a slip of paper either, but the proof that whoever asks for corn has need of it."

She took his hand between hers and held it to her heart. "It will be like coming to Egypt, and folks will say about you as Joseph did to his brothers, *'God did send me before you to preserve life.' "*

Jared laughed. "That will be after they're persuaded I'm not a witch!"

On the afternoon of the third day, when the corn was all harvested and they stood in the empty clearing with only the bundles of stalks about them, Jared took Jennet into his arms and kissed her.

"This is the last time I shall kiss you," he said tenderly.

"The last time?" she queried anxiously, clinging to him, for never once during the three days had Jared shown fear for the trial's outcome.

"Yes, the last time as a maid. The next time it will be as my betrothed."

She made no answer, for the clasp of her arms about him said more than many words.

But the time was short and even love must wait on justice. Jared glanced up at the sun. " 'Tis time I was starting," he said.

"And I'll follow soon," she promised. "I'll choose the most golden of all the ears and put them in a bag to bring with me to the Meeting House."

Jared left her then, with the Gray One standing near for her to ride down to the village. He went through the woods to wash at the brook and tidy himself after his work. Soon he was walking down the road, stopping at the Dunklees' on the way.

Eliza met him at the door. She was ready for the trial, dressed in her Sunday best. There was sympathy in her eyes and concern in her face.

"Jennet has a dress here, Eliza, that she brought with her from over the mountain," he began.

" 'Tis her wedding dress," Eliza said sadly, "and it looks now as if she may never wear it."

"See that she wears it today," Jared said, and then was off down the road with his easy stride.

Jared walked into the Meeting House as the clock was striking four. Randall Eveleth, the Justice of the Peace, was already in his place. He bowed to Jared, who took a seat beside him. The men that Ephraim Twiss had gathered began coming in. One by one they filed into their seats, and on their faces were written bitterness and anger dulled by waiting. Their womenfolk walked behind them silently. Then the curious flocked in until the room seemed hardly large enough to hold all who would be present. Near to where Jared sat, those who would speak for him arranged themselves–Dan True and the whole Dunklee family, down to the five-months-old babe. Jennet was not there.

Order was called, and Randall Eveleth stood up before the crowded Meeting House.

"Who brings a charge against Jared Austin?" he asked in the cool tone of impartiality.

"I do." Ephraim Twiss rose from his seat.

"We all do," the men sitting near him said.

"What is it?"

"Witchcraft proved and double proved," Twiss said, and then began the grim tale of the summer when all hope of any harvest had been frozen to death. He left out nothing, and the frost and the storms, the lost crops and ruined lands were attributed to Jared.

When he had finished, Mr. Eveleth said quietly, "I have heard reports about weather like this in many parts of the world–England, Ireland, and France. These conditions have been widespread. There must be further proof that the accused is as you say. Who's next?"

The bearded man rose, and with an oath brought forth his assertion that Jared Austin had bewitched his wife, for on the days when she would churn, a woodchuck never failed to sit on her doorstone and the butter always failed to come.

A murmur of incredulity ran through the group of onlookers.

"You believe that Jared Austin was the woodchuck?" Mr. Eveleth asked, his eyebrows raised.

"Aye, that I do." The bearded man sat down and looked at Ephraim Twiss.

Another man rose and swore to passing Jared on the road one day and upon reaching his barnyard, finding a litter of young shoats dancing on their hind legs. Going to the pump for water to pour on the bewitched animals, he found that no water would come; and going to the hearth for a hot poker, he found no fire there.

The listening crowd stirred, and Jared caught frowns of puzzlement on the faces of the men he knew to be honest farmers.

Mr. Eveleth heard them all. Some had much to say and some had little. Some swore that they had seen Jared in conversation with the Devil and some that the horse he rode was one of the Devil's shapes. Some referred to his stenciling as devilish writings that bewitched a household into doing his will, and some made mock of his lean body that felt neither cold nor hunger.

After each one, Mr. Eveleth gave a sober nod of dismissal. Finally he turned to those who would speak for Jared.

Dan True rose first. "The Hebrews had a scapegoat they laid their sins upon; today these men are trying to make Jared Austin accountable for their misfortunes. But he is a good man and though disaster has come near us, I take my Bible oath that he's had naught to do with the Devil."

John Dunklee stood up and in a husky voice said, "Jared Austin is my friend, and I'll call heaven to record that the good he does is from God. I've a fine heifer running in my fields this day that would not be there were it not for the care Jared Austin gave when it was stillborn."

There was an angry murmur among the men grouped near Ephraim Twiss when John Dunklee mentioned the heifer.

Eliza Dunklee rose and told how, when she was alone in the house and her time had come, Jared Austin had helped her babe into the world.

Mr. Eveleth nodded gravely. "Jared Austin," he said, facing the defendant, "you have heard the voices of these accusers. Have you ought to say for yourself?"

"Not in my own words, sir, but with your permission I'll ask the Psalmist to speak for me."

Mr. Eveleth agreed, and Jared moved over to where the Bible used on Sundays lay open on the lectern. He turned the pages to find his place, then read the words slowly, cherishing each one before he sent it forth. As he read, there were those whose lips trembled and those whose eyes grew moist, but there was not one who dared murmur against him.

"Mercy and truth are met together; righteousness and peace have kissed each other. Truth shall spring out of the earth; and righteousness shall look down from heaven." He paused, fixed his eyes on Ephraim Twiss, and then continued. *"Yea, the Lord shall give that which is good; and our land shall yield her increase. Righteousness shall go before him; and shall set us in the way of his steps."*

Jared sat down quietly, his face pale and his long thin fingers trembling. He looked toward the Dunklees, wondering what had kept Jennet from being with them; then he looked toward the door, longing for her presence.

Mr. Eveleth's cool glance went around the room. "Will anyone else speak for the accused?"

There was a stir at the entryway of the Meeting House. The door opened, and Jennet Thaxter, in a sky blue dress adorned with her own embroidery, came in. Her hair lay smooth and satin-shiny on her shoulders. Her face was wreathed in a smile like the face of a bride. With a quick, firm step she came down the aisle, bending only a little under the half-filled bag slung over one shoulder.

"Sir, I have this to say," she said, placing the bag on the floor. Opening it, she reached deep inside and took out a golden ear of corn. She held it high above her head, then let it fall back into the bag again.

There was a gasp among the people gathered in the Meeting House, as of a crowd thirsting in a desert land and seeing water at last.

"Whose corn have you there?" Mr. Eveleth asked.

"Jared Austin's, sir. He grew it this summer in a clearing too high for the frosts to reach; too sheltered for the winds to batter–and he grew it that all his neighbors might have meal in the winter and seed in the spring!" There was a proud glory in her face as she spoke, and on the lips of her mind were the words, "And the man who grew this corn is soon to be my wedded husband."

Mr. Eveleth reached into the bag to touch the corn for himself. He looked at it as a man might look at newly-mined gold. Then he faced the people solemnly. "The man who grew that corn in this starvation year is a Christian."

There was silence in the crowded room. Mr. Eveleth turned to Ephraim Twiss. "Have you anything further to say?"

Ephraim Twiss shook his head dully, and in his hard-lined face, shame was already erasing the marks of anger.

Mr. Eveleth turned to Jared. "Not guilty," he said; then he looked at Twiss again. "And you, Ephraim Twiss, must pay the cost of the trial."

Ephraim Twiss slowly nodded his head and slowly rose and walked down the aisle, followed by the other men. Soon there was no one left in the Meeting House but Dan True and the Dunklee family and Mr. Eveleth standing beside Jared and Jennet with the bag of corn between them.

Jared took Jennet's hand in his and looked up at Mr. Eveleth. "Sir, would you be so kind as to pronounce us betrothed? For that's what we're wanting to be."

Mr. Eveleth smiled and made the pronouncement, adding, "And what's more, I'll come this way a fortnight hence to bind the bonds of matrimony for you."

Eliza Dunklee let out a cry of joy and came forward to kiss Jennet and take Jared's hands in hers.

"Oh, Jared! So Jennet is the one, and I never knew, I never knew," she sobbed in her joy.

"You it was, Eliza, who bade me claim the thing I love," Jared said softly. "Don't you remember? That April night was not so long ago."

A full moon bent low in the sky and its mellow light tipped the spears of frost on the grass as Jared and Jennet stepped over the threshold of their house. Jared looked at the stencils he had drawn with such care upon the walls. The little hearts had been hung for him and Jennet after all, and the little bells had been waiting to ring for them.

Jennet smiled up at him, though the night air made a shiver run over her. "Beauty is a bright flame, Jared," she said.

"And a warm one too," he cried, catching her in his arms.